Three O'Clock
Séance

Three O'Clock Séance

An Inspector Rebecca Mayfield Mystery

JOANNE PENCE

QUAIL HILL PUBLISHING

Quail Hill Publishing

PO Box 64

Eagle, ID 83616

Visit our website at www.quailhillpublishing.net

First Quail Hill Publishing E-book: January 2016

First Quail Hill Print Book: January 2016

Second Quail Hill Print Book: August 2018

First Quail Hill Large Print Book: August 2018

ISBN: 978-1-949566-18-5

Chapter 1

On Tuesday afternoon San Francisco Homicide Inspector Rebecca Mayfield did something completely out of character. She left work early and went home.

Homicide had been eerily quiet for the past two weeks. Murders happened, but they were all gang-related, which meant the Gang Task Force took the lead. Homicide did its part, but the Task Force usually knew who the shooters were before the body was even cold. She had cleared so many cases and finished so much paperwork, she could see the top of her desk. Not all of it, but most. That was progress.

Her apartment was in a building three stories tall. The home of Bradley Frisk, the building's owner, made up the entire top floor, in what San Franciscan's called a "flat." The middle flat was where Kiki Nuñez lived, a forty-something year old divorcee who owned her own exclusive spa. The bottom street-level floor consisted of a two-car garage, and behind it, facing the backyard, was

Rebecca's small apartment. Originally it had been a storeroom. A tunnel-like breezeway led along the outside of the garage from the street to the backyard.

As Rebecca opened her apartment door, Spike, a ten-pound Chinese Crested Hairless/Chihuahua mix, greeted her by jumping on his hind legs and spinning in circles. He was a neat little guy, although definitely strange looking with tufts of white hair on the top of his head, ears, tail, and from the knees down, but hairless and spotted in between. She had found him shivering in fear at a crime scene and decided to keep him when the pound declared him not adoptable because he tried to bite anyone, other than her, who attempted to pet him. Since he'd watched his owner die in a shootout where over forty rounds of bullets had been fired, she understood his wariness.

After feeding Spike and relaxing a bit, Rebecca decided to see what Kiki was up to. She could go for some girl talk. And maybe a little wine. She went into the yard and took the steps up to Kiki's place and knocked on her back door.

Kiki didn't answer, so Rebecca went up one

more flight to the top floor and knocked on Bradley's back door. He wasn't home either.

Clearly, everyone led a far more exciting life than she did.

Back in her apartment, she switched on her plasma, flat-screen television. Richie Amalfi, a sometime friend of hers, had sent it to her after her boxy, antique one had been destroyed by a crazy Russian gang. He assured her it wasn't new, that it hadn't "fallen off a truck," and that she was more than welcome to it.

She wrestled with herself a bit, but then decided to keep it. Everything was so expensive in San Francisco that not even a homicide inspector's salary went very far. If it wasn't for overtime, she wasn't sure she could make it. And it was a really nice TV.

After eating a sandwich for dinner, she switched it off. Television held no interest that night.

She was currently dating Ray Torres, a patrol officer. He was a nice fellow, but this week he was working the night shift. She thought about sending him a text to ask him to stop by if he was cruising the neighborhood. It wasn't his territory, but cop cars did travel far afield at times.

The more she thought about it, she didn't feel like seeing him either. She could only stand hearing so much about MMA wrestling.

A name flitted across her mind, the name of a person who always seemed to make life a lot more exciting when he was near. But that ship had sailed. Good riddance.

She shut off the TV and took Spike out to the back yard to play. For his "needs," due to Rebecca's sometimes long and always irregular hours, he was small enough that he used a kitty litter box kept in the bathroom.

The back yard was nothing but a concrete square surrounded on all sides by three-story tall buildings. In its center, the landlord had placed a large raised flower bed with a built-in bench along its edges. Shade-loving begonias, impatiens, hydrangeas and ferns gave the yard color and warmth.

Rebecca sat on the bench and was playing fetch with Spike, throwing a little red ball for him, when she heard a doorbell. At the end of the breezeway, facing the street, was a locked door to keep strangers from wandering into the back yard uninvited. The bell beside that door was wired to ring in her apartment.

No one ever rang that bell unless she was expecting someone. And she wasn't.

Given her irregular hours, her friends always texted or called before coming to visit.

She figured it was just some kids playing around, but then the bell rang again, and she heard knocking on the door.

She walked through the breezeway, opened the door, and gaped. The embodiment of her earlier thoughts stood before her. "Richie."

"Hey," he said with a smile. "Good to see you. How you been? Can I come in?"

She frowned, not wanting any part of this bizarre hale and hearty greeting. The last time she'd spent any real time with him was two months earlier when he'd stepped in to help when she found herself in the cross hairs of the deadly Russian gang that wrecked her TV. He ended up getting shot for his efforts. She had thought, after all that, they'd reached a new level in their relationship, but when his arm healed, he had made no effort to see her. Except for a couple of days surrounding the wedding of his cousin, Angie Amalfi, to one of Rebecca's coworkers, Paavo Smith, he'd been AWOL. "What do you want?"

Spike peered around her leg, saw Richie and started jumping in circles, his tail wagging like crazy. Despite his usual wariness around strangers, Spike had taken to Richie almost from the first time the two met.

"Hey, little buddy." Richie bent down and petted him. "At least you're glad to see me."

She stepped back, letting him and Spike reconnect. Richie was dressed casually in a light gray sport coat, pink shirt, no tie, and black slacks. She remembered once reading that a man had to be confident in his masculinity to wear a pink shirt. That described Richie.

"Okay, come in," she said.

Spike nearly jumped into his arms, and Richie carried him into the yard, making over him the whole time.

She sat back down on the flower bed bench. She knew he had heard her question. She waited for him to answer it.

He sat beside her, then picked up Spike's red ball and tossed it. Spike scrambled, grabbed the ball and brought it back. Richie petted and praised him, then tossed it again. She watched Spike, but even more, she watched Richie.

He was about four years older than her 35 years and stood about an inch taller than her 5'10" height. His hair, worn long enough to show its waves, was black as soot, although the temples held a few strands of gray. His eye color seemed to change from being as black as his hair, to showing flecks of light brown and even green in sunlight. But more than any of that, he had an expressive face, and could say as much with his eyes as with his words. She found him good-looking, but she had dated plenty of handsome men, and she was surrounded by great looking cops all day long at her job.

Maybe whatever strange fascination he held for her was because she couldn't figure him out.

Finally, he said, "Something's going on that needs looking into."

So he was here because of her job. What else

had she expected? "If it's not a dead body, it's not my area."

He caught her gaze. "But it is. Only it hasn't been declared a murder. Not even a suspicious death. That's the problem."

None of what he was saying made sense. "If the death isn't suspicious, why are you concerned? Are you now an expert in causes of death?"

"As a matter of fact, there's been more than one death; more than one body." His jaw tightened as he added, "And now my mother's friend is involved with the guy who may be behind it. Whatever is going on, he makes my teeth hurt. I know he's crooked, but I can't find anything on him. I don't like it."

At the thought of Richie's mother, Rebecca couldn't help but grimace. The woman had taken an instant dislike to her. "Carmela doesn't miss a thing. I'm sure she can take care of herself and her friend."

"Usually, that's true," Richie said. "But she has one real big weak spot."

"Other than you?" At his frown, she asked, "What is it?"

"Ghosts, spirits, and anything that has to do with talking to the dead."

Carmela was a spiritualist? She'd never met anyone more down-to-earth and practical. "Your dead bodies don't have anything to do with ghosts, do they?"

He hesitated a moment, even looking a bit embarrassed. "Sort of. The guy I'm worried about is one of those 'I-talk-to-dead-relatives-of-people-who-give-me-money' con artists."

This was getting better by the minute. "Are you saying he's a medium?"

"You got it. He calls himself a psychic medium for the dead."

She was appalled. "Why, in heaven's name, have you come to me about this?"

He looked at her as if her question was crazier than Carmela's friend. He jumped to his feet—Richie never could sit still for long. "Who else was I supposed to go to? Tell me. Who?" He spread his arms wide—he was definitely Italian. "If I'd gone straight to Homicide, Calderon and Bo Benson would have laughed and then tossed my ass out of there; Paavo's now part of the family so I don't see him or his partner interviewing my mother, who happens to be his wife's aunt; and Bill Sutter would rather sleep at his desk than do any actual work. That leaves you."

She folded her arms. "Nice to know I'm your last choice."

At that, he grinned—he had a really nice smile—and sat down next to her again, his shoulder touching hers. "Actually, you're my first choice, but I had to think of some reason why the other guys wouldn't work."

It was a struggle not to smile back. She shifted away from him, hands on thighs, and took a deep breath. "Look, the last time I was involved in an off-the-books case with you, I nearly lost my job—"

"Your case, not mine," he pointed out.

"It was only because I had a flawless record, and I'm the only female in Homicide, that I wasn't fired or demoted. I'm not going to risk it again by going off looking for some spiritualist charlatan that you're implying may be a murderer."

"You also kept it because you're one of the best detectives in the department, and everyone knows it," he said. His gaze slowly took in her face from the broad forehead to the almost pointed chin. "I've missed you, by the way."

His praise, words, and warm scrutiny left her momentarily speechless until she decided he was simply trying to worm his way into her good graces so she'd help him. "You're wasting your time dealing with Homicide. Or me. You should find a private eye."

"What if I'm right, Rebecca? How many more people—alone and elderly—will he kill before he makes a mistake and the police go after him?"

"That's a low blow." He knew she had a strong sense of duty, and that she foolishly (in his opinion) thought she somehow might make a difference, for the better, in other people's lives. He was playing on that sense, a sense she saw as strength, and he saw as weakness. Another of their major differences.

"It's true." He got up, picked up Spike's red ball and, to Spike's delight, tossed it. He turned to her. "I'm here because this situation worries me. I hope I'm wrong, but I don't think so. At least come with me tonight to see this guy's act."

"Why in the world would I do that?"

"Because it's a long story, and I think it'll all make much more sense after you've seen the guy I'm talking about. Then you can decide to ignore me or not. His performance starts at eight in a little theater out in the Richmond district—the kind of safe area his audience, people like my mother and her friend, feel comfortable going to."

She had truly vowed to never again have anything to do with Richie Amalfi.

But then, she didn't have anything else to do that evening.

And besides, she was feeling bored and more than a little intrigued at the thought of seeing a psychic medium in action. It had nothing to do with Richie.

Chapter 2

Rebecca changed into a pale mauve skirt, a black pullover with a scoop neckline, and black heels with a sexy ankle strap. She removed the pony tail band to free her long blond hair, added a little jewelry, a little make-up, a splash of perfume, and she was done.

Eat your heart out, Amalfi.

The way Richie eyed her as she walked into the living room, he may have been doing just that. "You clean up real good, Inspector."

"Yeah, well, I'm sure you'll let me know if I still have dirt on my face or hayseeds between my teeth."

He chuckled as they left the apartment.

She sat in the passenger seat of his Porsche 911 Turbo. The light scent of his after shave reminded her of other times she'd been in his car, times she preferred to forget.

Richie told her a bit more as he drove across town. Sandor Geller was the psychic's name.

Rebecca wondered if he was any relation to Yuri Geller who people had believed could bend spoons with his mind until it was shown that magicians could do everything Geller did. But Yuri Geller continued to insist he was legit, and to this day had a large, loyal following with books and television shows. Sandor may have decided to use the name since many people already knew it. Or, he may have been born with it.

In the past, Rebecca had observed that Richie had a good sense about people, what some might call intuition, while she felt about as intuitive as a tsetse fly. He clearly believed something strange was going on with this so-called psychic wannabe, and logic told her he might be right.

The building where the event would take place was large enough to be impressive, but nowhere near the size of the downtown halls that psychics such as John Edward, James Van Praagh, Rosemary Altea, Sylvia Browne, or George Anderson might have needed for their sell-out crowds.

Although Rebecca would never in a million years admit it to Richie or anyone else, she was familiar with those people. She first became interested in paranormal phenomena while in high school. She even went to a ghost hunt on Halloween at the enormous, spooky Old Penitentiary back home in Boise. They did a few things to entertain the customers, but not one ghost appeared. She had watched *The Amityville Horror* any number of times, and read everything she could get her hands on about Ed and Lorraine Warren, demonologists who were involved in that and a number of other cases.

But by the time a movie involving the Warrens, *The Conjuring,* came out, Rebecca was already a cop. The evil and demonic acts she saw in real life made Hollywood's view of them child's play by comparison. With her job, any interest in psychic phenomena, demons, and spirits had vanished along with her innocence.

The theater probably held some seven or eight hundred people in lightly padded fold-down seats and was quickly filling up. Richie found places for them in the middle of the audience. He didn't want to be too far back and miss anything.

Before the show began, a skinny, pale young

man, his brown hair pulled into a man-bun, came onto the stage. He introduced himself as "Mr. Geller's assistant, Lucian," and then insisted everyone turn off their cell phones and not take pictures or make recordings. Next came a parade of people with stories of how Sandor Geller connected them with dead friends and loved ones.

Nothing like priming the pump, Rebecca thought.

Finally, the lights dimmed, a hush fell over the audience, and as recorded music blared, Sandor Geller walked out on stage wearing a purple cape and silver turban with a jeweled pin holding a peacock feather sticking straight up from it. He strutted around the stage while most people cheered, and a few hooted and laughed.

"Is this a joke?" Rebecca asked. "Who would ever take this jerk seriously?"

"Keep watching," Richie whispered.

"*I am Sandor Geller,*" the guy bellowed in a loud, deep voice. "*Or ...*"

He removed the turban, the cape, and the tear-away tuxedo suit under it and tossed everything to his assistant, Lucian. Despite the gasps from some in the audience as he tore away his suit, he hadn't turned the show into a Chippendale male stripper routine. Instead, Geller stood before them in scruffy jeans and a cream-colored shirt with a wide collar and baggy sleeves. He rolled back the sleeves, ran his fingers through his hair to fluff it, and then flung open his arms, saying in a normal voice, "You can call me Sandy."

The audience roared its approval. Sandy held up a finger in a "one moment" gesture and took off his black dress shoes. Lucian ran out on stage and exchanged them for a worn pair of brown loafers. Sandy put on the loafers and heaved a loud sigh of relief. "Now I'm ready!" He gave a dimpled smile, to even more sustained applause. He looked about twenty years old, although Rebecca imagined he must be at least in his mid-thirties.

Women made up most of the audience, and "Sandy," as opposed to "Sandor" looked pretty darn cute with rakish hair, twinkling blue eyes, and those deep dimples. Rebecca now understood a good part of his appeal.

He began with humorous stories about performances in Los Angeles, Denver, and the day before in Las Vegas, explaining that he toured those areas at least once each month to meet with his followers. He added how glad he was to be "home" now, implying that his San Francisco audience was far more sophisticated than the rubes elsewhere. And that, as a result, the evening they would spend together would be far more important and satisfying to all of them.

Next, he gave a quick description of his childhood, of growing up a loner with no friends because of his psychic gifts. He did it in a way that caused the audience to care about and connect with him. They laughed at some of the stories, and he brought many people to tears with others, such as when he spoke of being with his grandmother as she was dying, and how he witnessed his long-deceased grandfather appear at her bedside. He described her joy at seeing her husband again, how she was then no longer afraid to die, and let herself go. He watched her spirit walk with her husband to the "other side."

Despite herself, Rebecca hung onto his every word. Although she'd had a youthful interest in psychic mediums, she'd never gone to one of their performances—the cost of them being a big factor. She grew up on a farm where money was in short supply.

Sandy abruptly stopped his ramblings in mid-sentence. "Oh, my God! Someone is here."

The audience froze, waiting, listening.

Sandy put his hand to his forehead. "He refuses to wait, but says he needs to talk now. I'm hearing a name. It seems to start with a D. Or is it a B? P? The letter T, perhaps?"

She leaned towards Richie. "What's this? Do spirits mumble or is 'Sandy' hard of hearing?"

Richie grinned. "The letters he should be hearing are P.O.S."

She chuckled and poked his arm with her elbow.

In answer to Sandy's question, several women waved their arms, stood up and shouted names like Debbie, Barbara, Pam, and Theresa.

Sandy studied them a moment, then in a hushed voice said, "He's saying another name. Ch … Chuck, is it?" The women shook their heads. "Charles!" he cried.

"Yes," one of the women called. "That's my

husband's name."

"Is he deceased?" Sandy asked.

"Yes, these past fifteen years." A spotlight found the stout woman with short white hair who was answering. She blinked hard from its brightness as, in answer to Sandy's questions, she said she was Barbara from Walnut Creek.

"Charles is here now, Barb. Oh, my. Was that his nickname for you? Barb?" Sandy asked, then, without waiting for her answer, said, "What would you like to say to him?"

Rebecca nearly tossed her cookies at the syrupy-sweet discourse that followed. Barbara, who was very shy, said little, but Sandy allowed himself to be the "vessel" through which Charles spoke. As Charles, his voice turned thin and slightly raspy, and his shoulders seemed to hunch up, while his head sank a bit in the way of an older man. "Charles" told how much he loved and missed Barbara. He spoke of her as a young, beautiful bride, of their vacations together, her wonderful cooking, and most of all, the way they had loved and made love. Somehow, Rebecca was sure Barbara and Charles didn't have the passionate sex life Sandy conjured up, but "Barb" wasn't about to admit it before all those people. The woman put her hands to her cheeks and blushed bright red, but her gaze was filled with complete love … for Sandy.

Rebecca now understood the loose cream-colored shirt and longish hair. He looked like Lord Byron or the hero of some historical romance novel.

She could hardly suppress a giggle, but most of the audience was completely enthralled, many in tears, and even more with expressions of undying adoration, just like Barbara.

"He's gone now," Sandy whispered, then dropped to his knees with a face so filled with sadness he looked like part of a medieval painting of the crucifixion.

Rebecca couldn't stop a derisive snort, and quickly put her hand to her nose, pretending it was a cough as murder flashed in the eyes of the women seated near her—her murder.

Barbara, who was now fully engulfed in tears, worked her way to the aisle, wiping her cheeks and nose with her hands as she went. Sandy's bodyguards acted as if they were going to try to stop her, but the blatantly compassionate Sandy insisted they let her pass and that she be allowed to approach him, a gesture to make the audience love him even more, no doubt. He stood as she ran into his arms, and they hugged. Rebecca suspected "Barb" was thinking more about Sandy than poor dead Charles.

Sandy quickly sent her back to her seat.

The evening went on that way, although later encounters weren't nearly as dramatic. Still, Rebecca knew the majority of the audience believed he was truly psychic. He had a way of working the crowd that, to a skeptic like Rebecca, came across as plastic, phony, and with all the subtlety of a hand grenade. Yet, no one in attendance seemed to notice.

He said things like "I see a body of water. Does that mean anything to anyone?"

Rebecca would have loved to point out that since they were in San Francisco, with water on three sides, it certainly should have meant something.

"Do you have a cat? A dog?" Someone in any

large audience could usually answer affirmatively to that one. But he also had many misses, and, to help keep them hidden, he spoke so quickly it was like a multiple-choice exam with untold possible answers. Tossing out a number of possibilities meant at least one would solicit a "Yes!"

Sandy would then zero in on that "yes" and ask that person to stand. He then continued with questions or statements, rapid-fire, until he hit something that would make the person say "Yes!" again.

Sometimes, nothing seemed to work and the person standing kept shaking his or her head. Before he allowed that to go on very long, Sandy would notice someone else in the audience nodding, and immediately swivel around to focus all his attention on the new person, abandoning the earlier one, who would be left there feeling foolish, and eventually sit down. A loser.

He ended the evening with a tear-jerking connection with someone who had recently lost a beloved cat. Thank God, Rebecca thought, Sandy didn't meow for her.

Then, exactly one hour after he stepped onto

the stage, his performance was over.

"That's it?" Rebecca asked. "Seventy-five bucks each for that B.S.?"

"You got it," Richie said. "And now we can buy Sandy's book *and* the T-shirt. And we can become Sandoristas for only $6.99 a month."

"You sound like an infomercial."

"Well, you do get the newsletter if you sign up," he chided.

"Such a deal!" Rebecca quipped. But then, as they walked through the lobby where people were buying the Sandorista bling, her smile vanished. "Wait a minute. That Sandorista name sounds familiar."

"It sounds like Sandinistas, but—"

"That's it!" she said.

"I know, but—"

"No, no. Let's get out of here." They left the theater and headed towards Richie's car when Rebecca continued. "The name came up in a case Sutter and I worked a while back."

He gave her a smug look. "If you and Sutter were involved, that means someone was dead, just as I was saying."

"Saying 'I told you so' is not an attractive trait," she said. "Besides, it could be nothing."

"Or something. Is it a case you cleared, or is it still open?"

"I can't remember which one it was. I think it was a throwaway line, something we saw and dismissed, but I'm just not sure."

"Probably still open, then. We should check it out."

"We?" She lifted her eyebrows.

"Sure. I've already gotten you this far," he said.

"This *far*? I haven't actually said I was interested, you know."

Rebecca slowed her steps as she noticed an attractive woman in a green coat with a fur collar, her auburn hair cut in a shiny smooth chin-length bob, leaning against Richie's car smoking a cigarette. When the woman saw the two of them, her eyes went to Richie. She dropped the cigarette on the sidewalk and stepped on it. Then walked away.

"Was she waiting for you?" Rebecca asked as they continued to his car.

Richie shook his head. "I think she was just someone having a smoke. Anyway, now I see the future."

"You do?"

"It has you and me, together, working on the cold case you were talking about. Time for a trip to Homicide."

She shook her head at the thought of allowing him to work a cold case with her. Sandy wasn't the only one around who was delusional.

Chapter 3

Rebecca saw nothing illegal or fraudulent in Geller's act. It was pure theater, a performance—a magic trick—and not a particularly clever one. The people who believed in him did so because they wanted to and perhaps found it comforting. Sandy was a good performer, throwing out questions, ideas, and images at such a fast pace that the people listening were overwhelmed. He never said anyone should "believe" anything—he carefully kept saying what "he" saw or heard or felt. It was up to the audience to decide how much credence to give to his remarks.

Richie drove to Homicide and parked in the employee lot of the Hall of Justice, a massive gray, bland building devoid of design that took up one side of Bryant Street between Sixth and Seventh. They rode the elevator to the fourth floor where the Homicide bureau was located.

The department was empty. Only the night lights were on, casting a dim florescent glow over the large room, one bulb flickering.

Rebecca didn't bother to turn on all the overheads since she had a lamp on her desk, the one she used when she worked long into the night. She switched it on now.

"Why don't you tell me all you know about Sandor Geller and his Sandoristas," Rebecca said as she sat and began thumbing through her files of open cases.

Richie slid the guest chair to her side to better see what she was looking at. "My mother told me it all started with her best friend Geraldine Vaccarino. Geri, as she's called, had a sister, Betty, who was quite a bit older. She lived in Los Angeles, had never married, and was estranged from the family. Geri didn't know until about a year after it happened that Betty had died."

"What was Betty's full name?" Rebecca picked up a pen.

"Elisabetta Faroni." He spelled out Betty and Geri's full names for her. "After getting over the shock of her sister's death, Geri started to think about Betty's money. I don't know if you've had much experience with Italian families and money, but believe me, Geri would have started to think about it by the next day, if not sooner. She wondered where Betty's money and belongings had gone. She especially remembered an antique sewing machine from the old country that had been their mother's. It was built into a fancy wooden cabinet and used no electricity. The sewer worked a pedal under the machine."

"I've never seen such a thing," Rebecca said.

"If a person had one of those in good working order these days, it'd be worth something, so Geri started to look into it."

"Uh huh."

"And since Betty died intestate, you know, without a will, Geri couldn't find anyone who had any idea of where the money went. The landlord said he gave her things to Goodwill after no one claimed them for several months, but who knows?"

"So how is Sandor Geller involved?" Rebecca asked.

"Because one minute, Betty had money and savings, and the next, she didn't—or so it seemed to the family. One of Geri's sons drove her down to Los Angeles where she talked to Betty's neighbors to see what they knew." He took a deep breath, and his next words were spoken with a conspiratorial edge. "Geri learned that Betty had been introduced to Geller by a friend of hers who had gone to his séances for years. And then, one day, that friend was found dead. Betty was inconsolable.

"That, and family hints and silences, make me think she and her girlfriend were more than just friends, if you get my meaning. But my mother's generation rarely talked about such things, especially about family. Still, my suspicion could explain Betty's estrangement from them. Anyway, Geller calmed her down and let her talk to her friend during a séance. Betty claimed they spoke of things only the two of them knew about, but you've seen how clever Geller is suggesting something and letting his prey fill in the missing parts."

Rebecca was taken aback. "Prey?"

"Damned right," Richie said. "This guy took advantage of a lonely old lady, gained her trust, and took her money. Betty had become a confirmed believer in Geller's abilities and ended up broke."

"Or," Rebecca said, "you can look at it from Geller's viewpoint. People pay him money to take part in a séance. It's not up to him to go into their finances to be sure they can afford his sessions."

"True. But that's where this gets really weird. After Betty spent all her money on Geller's séances, she told a neighbor he was helping her with expenses."

Rebecca was stunned. "Geller gave her money?"

"Yes. And, she told the neighbor he'd done the same for her friend who'd died—the one who had introduced her to Geller in the first place."

"Could it be he's a good man who felt bad that the woman went so far overboard? Maybe, once he found out, he simply wanted to help."

"Yeah, he's a real prince among men." Richie apparently couldn't sit and stare at paperwork any longer. He got up and paced. "I'm telling you, something's wrong. But that's all background. It's what's going on now that worries me."

"Which is?"

"A few months ago, Geri learned Geller's now in San Francisco and she went to see his act. She kept going, and now she's convinced Carmela to join her. They claim they're going just to be entertained, but I don't buy it.

"Then, last week, Carmela and Geri went to a funeral of one of the women Geri would sometimes see at Geller's séances. The woman supposedly had money, a nice house in the Marina, but she died alone, suddenly, and her funeral was practically that of a pauper. She had no family or anything, and her whole life revolved around her séances with Geller. She was, in fact, one of the very first Sandoristas in San Francisco. All in all, to me, her story sounds too similar to Betty Faroni's to be a coincidence."

"Now I remember!" Rebecca opened a file cabinet drawer, rifled through it, then pulled out a folder and put it on her desk. "It's not a cold case, because it wasn't even a case."

She looked through the papers, then stopped at one of them and read it over quickly. "This is it. The deceased, Neda Fourman, was eighty-nine years old and had a heart condition. When the building manager found her dead in her apartment, we were called in. I remember Bill Sutter, who was working the scene with me, finding pamphlets about life after death, séances, and a group called the Sandoristas. At first he thought she was involved in Nicaraguan politics—as in San-*din*-istas. It was actually pretty funny."

At Richie's expression, she said, "Death-cop gallows humor, what can I say?"

He grinned at that and then stood and leaned over her shoulder to look at the file with her.

"Anyway," she continued, "the M.E. checked her over, and we ruled it a death by natural causes."

"I see," Richie murmured as he skimmed through the paperwork.

She found his nearness unsettling and scooted to one side. "I have a couple of contacts in the LAPD, and I'll see if they saw anything at all questionable about the deaths of Betty Faroni and her friend. They might even have something on Geller." She shut the file, and he straightened. "Time to go."

Richie drove her back to her apartment and then walked her to the door by the garage that led to the breezeway. There, he stopped.

"Good night, Rebecca," he said. "Thanks for looking into all this."

She nodded. "No problem. You're being a

good son, looking out for your mother's friend."

"I look out, as much as I can, for everyone I care about," he said, his voice and eyes soft.

She quickly unlocked the door and then stepped into the breezeway before she faced him again. "Good night. I'll let you know if I find out anything."

She shut the door and waited until she heard the Porsche's engine start, and then, with a sigh, she headed for her apartment.

Chapter 4

The next morning, Richie picked up his phone to call his friend Shay, aka Henry Ian Tate III, aka HIT-man, with information about Neda Fourman: age, address, and date of death. He'd gotten the data as he leaned over Rebecca in Homicide last night. Thinking about being that close to her, alone, the lights dim … it had been all he could do not to pick up where they'd left off some months ago in his living room, the first and only time he'd ever seriously kissed her. He might have given her a peck on the cheek in greeting or whatever from time to time, but that day, in his living room, now *that* was a kiss.

Hell. Who knew he'd have such thoughts while in a Homicide bureau? His friends would snicker.

He had realized back then that he was starting to fall for her and broke it off. She was the type of woman a guy could get serious about, which made her the last type he wanted in his life.

And since she'd made it clear she didn't care to ever get serious about him, things were cool between them. Cool in the good sense.

That was why he was able to ask her to help him find out about this modern day Harry Houdini. They were simply friends, and this was strictly business, quiet nights in Homicide notwithstanding.

He made the call. Shay picked up, and Richie gave him the information. He didn't even need to say what he wanted done with it. Shay would know. Talk about psychic—the guy was spooky, and it wasn't because of any mind-reading ability.

Shay liked to say the moniker "HIT-man" referred to his prowess as a computer hacker, but he was also a deadly shot, military-sniper level, and he owned a battery of fire arms. Rumor had it he had an MBA from the Wharton School of Business. But then, there were a lot of rumors about Shay, including that he'd been in the CIA. Richie was one of the few people who knew the truth—he and Shay had been friends for years—but at times Shay's eyes held such icy coldness that even Richie wondered if there weren't parts of the story he didn't know.

The one thing Richie was certain of, was that Shay was too damned smart to be doing hacking, or worse, for a living.

But right now, it was Shay's hacking skills he needed. Shay would be able to find out things about Neda Fourman's life that not even Homicide could learn. And if "call me Sandy" had anything to do with it, Shay would find that out as well.

o0o

That same morning, Rebecca went through her notes about Neda Fourman. The review confirmed that there was no reason for her and Sutter to have questioned Neda's death as anything but natural. She was simply an old woman who'd had a heart attack.

Rebecca called her contacts in the Los Angeles Police Department to find out what she could about Betty Faroni's death. There again, a heart attack, no question about it. They also had nothing on Sandor Geller.

Rebecca wondered if she really wanted to pursue this, or just drop it. On the one hand, she had no case. Despite what might or might not have happened in Los Angeles, Neda Fourman's death appeared as natural as any elderly person's with a heart condition. And for that matter, so did Betty Faroni's.

But, what if Richie was right? There could be four old ladies all biting the dust a wee bit earlier than nature intended: not only Neda Fourman and Betty Faroni but also the unnamed woman Richie simply referred to as "Betty's girlfriend," and, possibly, the woman with the funeral fit for a pauper last week.

Although she was probably wasting her time, Rebecca picked up the phone and got through to Geller's secretary—a woman who sounded awfully cheerful for someone who worked around séances and, supposedly, the dead. Rebecca set up a meeting with Sandor Geller at 5 p.m. to discuss Neda Fourman who, at least, had once been her case.

At the appointed time, she went to his suite of offices in a Victorian-style house on Octavia Street near Vallejo. With its dark blue, purple and white gingerbread facade, a turret, and gabled windows, it looked like the perfect place to hold a séance.

The interior appeared to have been completely

renovated. Despite the Victorian furniture and faux oil lamps, it was set up like an office suite. The young, teeth-achingly perky receptionist led her from the parlor/reception area through a long corridor. On the left she passed open double doors that looked in on a generous room with a sofa, comfortable chairs, a large round table, and floor-to-ceiling bookcases filled with thick, serious-looking tomes. She wondered if Sandy held his group sessions there.

On the right, a row of offices gave insight to the size of Geller's business. Answering phone calls, emails, and requests for private meetings and public appearances seemed to require a couple of people full time, plus a bookkeeper.

All this was quite amazing for someone who held public performances at what was essentially an old, run-down theater smaller than many high school auditoriums.

At the end of the hall, the receptionist had her enter Geller's surprisingly sterile office, with a desk, and a small sitting area with a leather-covered sofa, chair, and coffee table. One modern painting filled with red and yellow lines and squares hung on a wall. As she took the chair by the sofa, the receptionist offered tea or coffee. She chose coffee.

Some ten minutes later, the doorknob turned, and Sandor Geller walked in. He was casually dressed in jeans and a blue pullover. She stood. As they introduced themselves, she saw he was older than he had appeared on stage where he wore make-up, with freshly washed and blow-dried hair that flopped youthfully about. Now, she could see age lines on his face, as well as weariness and redness in his eyes.

After preliminary pleasantries, he sat down on the sofa. "So tell me, Inspector, what can I do for you?"

She had to admit that even bloodshot, there was something intriguingly intense about his blue-eyed stare. "I'm looking into the death of a woman named Neda Fourman. Does her name mean anything to you, Mr. Geller?"

"Call me Sandy," he said, and then his face took on an expression of benevolence and dismay. "Ah, yes. Neda. She was a complete delight. An older woman, rather sickly, as I recall. But she died many weeks ago. That can't be why you're here, can it?" Then, as if he'd just been goosed, he sprang to his feet. "I just realized—you're in homicide. That doesn't mean there was something suspicious about her death, does it?"

She all but gawked at him. Was this guy always acting? Never before did a person she was interviewing need to remind himself that she was in homicide. "If there was nothing suspicious, I wouldn't be involved, Mr. Geller."

"Call me—"

"Sandy," she said quickly.

He sat again, his eyebrows knitted as if he were greatly troubled, and his voice barely above a whisper. "You aren't thinking she was murdered, are you?"

She didn't bother to answer. "What can you tell me about Ms. Fourman?"

"There's not really a lot for me to say. She was sweet, never married. But there was a man she had pined over for most of her life. Unfortunately, he had a wife, and so she simply loved him from afar. He was rather young when he died, only sixty, and she wanted to know if he had ever thought of her."

Rebecca was sure she knew the answer, but

still asked. "Had he?"

He smacked his hands together as if in prayerful joy and with a face filled with compassion said, "Oh, yes. I was able to contact him and we learned that he had been quite in love with her, but he never felt he was good enough for her. That was the reason he never acted on that love."

"When you say you 'contacted' him, you mean …?"

"Yes. On the other side."

"I see."

"It was all quite sad." Sandy looked almost as melancholy as he had on stage. "But once she learned how he'd felt, it actually made her happy. She knew she hadn't spent a lifetime being foolish."

"So she saw you once, and you were able to do all that for her?"

He chuckled. "Oh, Inspector! I can tell you know little about mediums. Think of it this way. Suppose, in an ocean filled with drops of water—for that's easily the number of spirits floating about out there in Heaven, or The Great Beyond, or the

Wheel of Life, or whatever you want to call it—someone comes and asks you to find one particular droplet. It would be impossible, wouldn't it?"

She nodded.

"Well, the good news is that the person doing the asking already has formed some sort of connection to that particular spirit. Think of it as a thread, a very thin thread, between their subconscious. It's my job to take hold of that thread and carefully pull it towards the person, doing my best not to break it. But often it breaks, and then we have to establish the connection once again another time."

"So her thread broke over and over?" Rebecca asked.

He laughed again. She was growing really sick of all his guffaws. "It sounds so crude when you put it that way. I'm afraid it did take a while to connect with him, but once his spirit came to her, through me of course, how very happy she was. She came back a number of times simply to meet with him again."

"I see. And what was his name?"

At that, Geller sent a text to his secretary to

find the Fourman file and bring it to him.

"While we're waiting for that information," Rebecca said, "tell me about the Sandoristas."

This time, his chuckle turned into a loud belly laugh. Something was seriously wrong with this guy. "A fellow who came to one of my group sessions in Los Angeles first used the term, and it stuck. That's all."

"But people join the group."

"They do. In great numbers. Very great numbers. Since I can't do everything, it's basically a self-help bunch. We have a monthly newsletter, and a number of local chapters throughout the country. Members get to know lots about each other while in the sessions, and before you know it, many become friends, sharing good times and bad with each other as well as each other's spirits. It's really quite remarkable."

"I would say so," Rebecca muttered.

"Yes, and it gets even better when their spirits become friends with each other as well. So now, people in the group know that their loved ones have company in the afterworld."

"Sounds like a party."

He began to laugh again, but abruptly stopped as he realized she was being sarcastic. "You aren't a believer." His voice held not only dismay but also peevishness.

"I'm afraid not. From what I've seen working Homicide, I think it's just fine that some murderers end up as nothing more than dust. And good riddance to them."

"That, my dear Inspector Mayfield, is what Hell is all about."

"Touché," she said.

He smiled and studied her a moment. "You intrigue me. You're a student of death, I'm a student of what happens after death. If you're free, I would love to carry on this conversation over dinner. I have a favorite French restaurant just a few blocks from here, and if you could accompany me, I would be most overjoyed."

He was on his guard here in the office, clearly acting, and she wondered if he might be more relaxed and open away from it. Also, talking to him did bring back some of her latent interest in psychic phenomena. "Overjoyed?" She couldn't help but tease at his use of the word. "How can I say no to that? And it is almost dinner time."

He gave her a broad, deep-dimpled smile. "Wonderful. It's also the cocktail hour, so I hope you'll consider yourself off duty by the time we get there."

"That's very possible," she said.

Just then, his secretary stepped into the room and handed him a folder.

He looked perplexed a moment and faced Rebecca. "Ah, what was it I was supposed to look up for you?"

"The name of the man Neda Fourman spent her life in love with. The one whose spirit came to her."

"Oh, yes. Poor old Neda." He opened the folder and flipped through several pages. "Here he is, Kenneth Neary."

She jotted down the name and then closed her notebook. "Done."

Chapter 5

Richie was at Big Caesar's nightclub talking to the bartender when one of his bouncers came up to him. Lenny Deeds was huge, with short blond hair and a neck about the size of Richie's waist. Richie had given the fellow a task to do that day, well before the club opened.

"I'm back, boss," Lenny said.

"Let's go to my office."

Once there, Richie shut the office door and offered Lenny a healthy shot of whiskey. Lenny downed it in one gulp.

"What do you have?"

Lenny handed over his digital camera with a telephoto lens. Richie began to go through the photos of everyone coming and going from Sandor Geller's offices on Octavia Street. In the few photos provided, he recognized no one until, in a photo taken late in the day, he saw a person he knew very well.

"Inspector Mayfield?"

"Yeah, boss. I knew you'd be interested in seeing that."

Richie was glad to know she took his suspicions seriously and was investigating the guy in person.

He continued through a couple more photos. When he reached the last one, his eyebrows rose. It was a photo of Mayfield and Geller leaving the office together. "What's this all about?" he grumbled.

"She left the office with him about a quarter to six. I figured nobody else would be going to see him if he wasn't even there, so I followed them. They walked to a cocktail bar a couple blocks away."

That was the last thing Richie was expecting. "You sure?"

"Yeah. I was getting thirsty, so I went in, too. She had a Mai Tai, and he had straight shots."

"When did they leave?"

"About seven."

So they were at a bar about an hour, Richie thought. Rebecca was probably quizzing the guy—maybe because she thought she'd get more out of him after he'd had a couple of drinks. "Okay, good. Thanks." He started towards the door to send Lenny back to his regular job since the club was about to open.

"Then they went over to a French restaurant," Lenny added squeamishly.

Richie froze mid-way across the office. "They *what?*"

"It's a small, pricey place, you know, and they sat near a window, so I was able to watch pretty easy. They was just getting the soup when I decided I better get over here for my job. It's one of those places where the food comes slow, you know, and a different kind of wine is brought out with each dish."

Richie ran a hand along the back of his head. "Christ, almighty."

"Yeah, I know," Lenny said, his mouth down turned. "There's really places like that. Kind of wasteful if you ask me, but—"

"I know there are." Richie realized his voice sounded a bit harsh and Lenny was only trying to help. "Anyway, how were they acting? Did it seem like they were talking business or what?"

Lenny gave him a strange look as he rubbed his chin. "I'm not sure, boss. I mean, I know she used to come here to see you and all."

"She never came here to see me," Richie assured him. "It was always about business."

"Oh." Lenny nodded. "Well, in that case, they were looking pretty damn chummy."

Richie poured himself a straight shot, this one even larger than Lenny's had been. "Tell you what. You go back over there and watch them. Let me know when they leave, and where they go. Or, I should say, where Inspector Mayfield goes. It's important."

"Sure, boss. But what about the club's front door?"

"I'll cover it myself if necessary," Richie raged. "Now, go!"

He slugged down the whiskey and when he looked up again, Lenny was gone.

oOo

Rebecca found Sandy to be a surprisingly interesting man. In the cocktail lounge, he told her a lot about himself—how he realized he had a gift as a child and all that he went through to build a reputation for himself.

He had met a number of famous psychics and demonologists, including the Warrens, and told Rebecca about them as people. She found it so fascinating that she was glad to continue the conversation over dinner.

Sandy suggested L'Auberge, which she knew to be pricey. "Dressed like this?" she asked, looking at both their jeans.

"They know me," he said.

She nodded.

The restaurant was small and dimly lit with a dark, rustic decor. They were seated at a candle-lit table by the window. She took a look at the French menu, no prices on hers, and decided to let him order for them both.

After their wine was served, Rebecca asked one of the primary questions she'd always had about séances: "For many years now, magicians have shown how easy it is to replicate feats performed at séances, so, why believe in them?"

Sandy steepled his fingers and smiled confidently. "Yes, it's true. Many mediums are fakes, but we must consider this: to use science, a study and subject devoted entirely to the material and physical realm to prove that something "extra-sensory" and non-physical exists, is ridiculous on its face.

These days, he explained, improved technology provided a number of techniques to measure and test psychic phenomena. But interestingly, teams of researchers and institutes have been unable to prove that psychic phenomena does *not* exist. Once they threw out those cases where fraud was found, and studied only what remained, while no case had yet been conclusively proven to be authentic, at the same time, no fraud was proven either.

"You're saying it's a standstill," Rebecca said.

"I'm saying it's impossible to scientifically prove the supernatural exists, which is why it's 'supernatural.' Also, mediums these days don't use those old magic tricks of the past. They're nice theater, but that's it."

"So what do you use?" she asked.

"Mostly channeling. The key is to naturally communicate with the spiritual world. In fact, I'd love to show you what I'm talking about. There's a house in Half Moon Bay where the spirit haunting it is very strong and even has a physical presence that many people have seen. I'm meeting a photographer there tomorrow to take a number of photos for a television special. I've had contact with the ghost that lives in the house several times. I haven't actually seen her, but I know she's been near. I'm sure, even a skeptic like you will feel her presence."

"Her?"

"Yes. The wife." Just then the waiter showed up with their first course, leek soup. "I need to be there about six tomorrow evening. We want some photos with the sun setting over the Pacific, and the ghost appears most often in the evening hours. Please say you'll come with me. I'll tell you all about it when we're there. It'll be an experience you'll never forget, I promise."

Scenes from old movies she used to thrill over, like *The Haunting of Hill House* and *The Turn of the Screw,* filled her head. "I'm in," she said. "No doubt about it."

oOo

Richie's evening was pure hell. He kept

expecting Lenny to get back to the nightclub any minute with news that Inspector Mayfield was home, tucked in bed, *alone*. But Lenny didn't.

Richie rarely touched alcohol when at work and often nursed one drink the entire evening—a gin and tonic without the gin. But as more time passed, the more his imagination went into overdrive and he kept going back to his office for another shot.

Not that he cared that she was out with a stinking rich, world-famous jerk who was wining and dining her, trying to lure her to who-knows-where, to do who-knows-what. Richie didn't care about that at all. It wasn't as if he and Rebecca would ever work as a couple. Not with the kind of guy he was, and the kind of woman she was. Oil and water had nothing on them.

His only concern was that she might be out with a psychotic killer. And he was the one who put her onto the smarmy SOB.

Midnight had come and gone before Lenny returned, his feet aching. He'd had to abandon his look-out vehicle because after the dinner, Mayfield and Geller went walking. They kept stopping in art galleries all around Union Square and ended up at a bistro where they drank Irish coffees before finally getting into a cab.

"A cab?" Richie asked, his fingers curling into fists. He had half a mind to send Lenny through a nearby window, but he knew better than to shoot the messenger. "Where did they go?"

"I don't know, boss. No more cabs come along. By the time I got one, they was gone. I had the driver take me back to my car."

As Richie fumed, Lenny swore he never saw two people who could walk and talk so damn much. "They got my corns acting up," he said, kicking off his shoes and reaching for a two-holed stocking foot to rub.

"You. Lost. Her." Richie's head was ready to explode.

Lenny looked scared. "I did my best, boss. Really. I tried! I went to the spot where the Inspector left her SUV, and it was gone. So either it got stole, or they took the cab back there and maybe she got in her car and went home. Or maybe followed him to his place. I don't know."

Soon after that, Richie's friend Vito showed up

at the club. Richie suspected someone had called him to come and drive Richie home. None of his employees were willing to try to tell him what he could and couldn't do—such as, he couldn't drive his car after getting shit-faced thinking about Rebecca Mayfield hanging out with a charismatic, handsome, and probably deviant, psycho psychic.

Vito, however, could do it. Vito Grasioso, one of Richie's closest friends, was brawny and square-shaped, except for his head which was smaller at the top than along his jaw, where rolls of fat had sunk. He had receding black hair, hang-dog eyes, and always wore a tan car coat with bulging pockets. No one, including Richie, was sure what he carried in them.

Richie tried arguing with Vito, but quickly realized he was in no shape to do anything but obey his friend's advice to accept a ride home. And to try to forget about Rebecca Mayfield.

Chapter 6

At Homicide the next morning, Rebecca picked up a folder on one of her cases, but all she could think about was Sandy Geller. Sure, he might be a crook, but he was also a fount of information. The subject, real or not, had her hooked, and she wasn't too sure that was a good thing.

"Morning," Lieutenant James Philip Eastwood, chief of the Homicide bureau, said as he passed her desk, jarring her out of her reverie. He was impeccable, as always, his shirt starched to a seemingly uncomfortable level, and his thick silver-colored hair formed into a small pomp above his forehead.

"Good morning, sir," she said, then hunched low over the open folder.

Only seven hours to go before she left work to meet Sandy. She couldn't deny excitement at seeing a haunted house with a psychic medium.

She had just begun to grow interested in the case folder in front of her when Homicide's secretary, Elizabeth, called to tell her she had a visitor in the front office.

That was odd, Rebecca thought, as she headed that way.

Standing in the office was a tall blond fellow, probably in his mid-thirties. The cut of his hair, his suit, and his stance told Rebecca one thing: FBI.

"I'm Inspector Mayfield," she said.

"Brandon Seymour, FBI." He showed his badge, and they shook hands. "Can we talk in private?"

"What's this about?" she asked.

"I don't want to meet in an interview room," he said. "I think you'd prefer more privacy."

He obviously knew that mirrors in interview rooms were one-way glass, and that conversations could be piped into other rooms, but his comment still baffled her. "I might want privacy?"

He didn't answer.

"This way." She led him to a small unused conference room. He sat on one side of the long table, Rebecca on the other. "Now, what's going on?"

"Do you know this woman?" he showed her a

photo of the red-haired woman she saw at Richie's car the other night after Geller's theater performance.

"No."

"Have you ever seen her before?"

"The hair makes her look like someone I may have seen."

"Where?"

"I'm not sure."

He had the typical flat expressionless style of FBI agents. She wondered if it was beaten into them at Quantico. Crack a smile and get bamboo slivers shoved under your fingernails.

"The only reason you noticed her was that she was waiting by Richard Amalfi's car when he was with you."

"Oh, really? Does the FBI do mind reading now?"

"You saw Amalfi signal her to leave."

"What the hell is going on?" she demanded.

"Her name is Claire Baxter. She's an art dealer, and lately she's been selling gold jewelry that came from Nimrud."

"From where?"

"Nimrud," he repeated louder, as if that would help. "It was a city in northern Iraq some twenty-eight hundred years ago. After it was excavated by archeologists, the artwork and materials found there were sent to museums around the world. Gold jewelry from tombs of some queens of Assyria were stored in Baghdad, and when the museum there was looted after the fall of Iraq in 2003, it was feared lost. But then, in 2006, over six hundred pieces of gold jewelry, precious stones and ornaments were found in a vault in the central bank. We've now learned that a number of those artifacts have since fallen into the hands of the Islamic State, ISIS, as museums have been looted by them and others throughout the region. According to briefings I've had from antiquities experts, the plunder and sale of ancient artifacts from Syria and Iraq has become big business and has helped create a seven billion dollar black market."

"Seven billion? That's incredible."

"But true. We've now received word that someone is trying to sell eight of the gold pieces. Claire Baxter is that seller."

"How do you know that she's selling this 'Nimrud' gold?" Rebecca asked. "Or that the pieces are even legitimate? I've heard a lot of fakes are also flooding the market."

"We've got proof the pieces aren't fakes. The irony is, it's Europeans and Americans who are buying this stuff, sending our money to fund terrorists."

"I see," she said with a grimace.

He nodded in agreement. "Fortunately, we have some people, known collectors, who care more about preserving the artwork than in increasing their own collections. One of them, a wealthy Iraqi who lives in San Francisco, saw two Nimrud bracelets and a necklace. He alerted Interpol, and they contacted our field office in San Francisco. I've been watching Baxter. She's keeping low. Too low. In fact, the only person I've seen her spend any time with is Amalfi. He's also hard to get close to. But then I saw you with him. When I tracked you down, I learned you're probably the last person we'd ever have to worry about being involved in anything like antiquities smuggling. So I'm hoping you can help us."

"I don't see how," she said. "And I can't believe Richie's involved in anything like that."

"'Richie,' is it?"

"That's what he uses."

Seymour allowed his mouth to wrinkle ever so slightly. "From what I've heard, 'Dick' would be more accurate."

She said nothing.

He cleared his throat. "We want you to find out everything *Richie* knows about all this."

"That's a waste of time," she said firmly. "He's not interested in art—illegal or otherwise." *Or was he? Claire Baxter was an attractive woman ...*

"You sound pretty sure of that," Seymour said.

She shook off her prior thought. "I know him and some of his family."

"Are you in a relationship with him?" Seymour looked a bit surprised even as he asked.

She pursed her lips. "God, no. Nothing like that. I'm not sure you'd even call us friends."

Seymour nodded. "Acquaintances. That makes more sense. That's what I assumed looking at your profiles."

"And?" she asked.

"We want to know what Claire Baxter and Amalfi are up to. And we think you're the best person to find out for us."

She had asked Richie time and again what he did to make money before taking over Big Caesar's nightclub, but he never told her. Her voice went as flat as Seymour's. "Is there any proof Richie is involved in something illegal?"

"We haven't come up with anything like that—not yet, anyway." She felt relief until he added, "But with guys like him, sooner or later, they make a mistake. Then, we'll be ready to step in."

She felt sick in the pit of her stomach. Had he really managed to fool her so completely?

Seymour gave her a strange look. "As far as we can tell, he's never crossed over the line in his dealings with people like Claire Baxter. But I'm sure you know he made his first million long before he took over the nightclub."

First million? "Right," she said. "He's talked about making money in real estate."

Seymour gave her a cold stare. "Maybe so, but

the real money comes from his other line of work. He's a fixer."

Chapter 7

Richie awoke to his doorbell ringing at ten o'clock that same morning. He had a raging headache. No, a hangover.

Now, awakened by the ringing and pounding on his door, he vaguely remembered Vito dropping him off at home last night. He blinked a couple of times. Looking around, he saw that he had managed to take off his shoes, but that was it, before collapsing face down on the bed. Apparently, he hadn't moved all night.

He stumbled out to the front door and opened it.

His other closest friend stood there. Shay was about as different from Vito as anyone could be. He was at least a half-foot taller, blond and aristocratic. He even dressed like some English lord, preferring a wardrobe of mostly what Richie learned were "heather" colored sport jackets—what the hell kind of color was heather?—and with it, he usually wore a cravat (another word from Shay) tucked into a white shirt.

On top of that, women claimed the guy was movie-star handsome. The first time Mayfield saw him, she'd looked like a victim of lockjaw the way her mouth gaped open. But then she got to know him, and he didn't look so hot to her anymore.

Shay didn't date. Not women or men. Richie had no idea what was up with that, and the one time he asked about it, he got such a cold stare he thought his liver would turn into a block of ice and he'd drop dead on the spot. He never asked again.

"What the hell happened to you?" Shay asked as he walked into the house.

Richie just shook his head and went off to the bathroom.

After a hot shower and clean clothes, he felt a little more human except for the headache. He went out to his kitchen, a bright—too bright this morning—good-size room with granite counter tops and all the latest appliances in stainless steel. Shay had already turned on the espresso machine and made him a triple shot Americano.

Richie sat at the table, a bottle of Motrin at his side and coffee in hand. Shay had the good sense not to say a word until both kicked in.

After a second cup of coffee, Richie was able to talk to him. "What did you find out?"

Shay leaned back in the kitchen chair and studied Richie before speaking. Richie hated it when Shay did that. "Before I tell you what I found," Shay said, "what went down with you last night?"

Shay and Vito had been the two guys who pulled Richie out of his depression, including too much drinking and screwing around, after his fiancée was killed in an auto accident some four years earlier. "What happened last night was a big mistake, nothing else," Richie mumbled. "I was acting stupid. It won't happen again. That's a promise, okay? Now, what did you find?"

"First, Claire Baxter. Not only has the FBI talked to her a couple of times, they've started leaning on people who've worked with her over the years. It could get ugly. She's going to have to come clean with them, or leave. She can't keep playing both sides."

Richie nodded. He didn't really want to deal with Claire or her problems. He had enough of his own. "Okay. I'll talk to her. What else?"

"I got into Neda Fourman's bank records. It's weird. She did have money to start with. Over forty thousand dollars. Hardly a fortune, but enough, especially coupled with Social Security and her nurse's pension, to keep her in her own apartment and living well in her old age. But then, soon after Geller showed up in San Francisco, she started writing out checks to him. They were small to start with, but after she joined the Sandoristas, her checks grew in size—often, for five hundred dollars. Some months she wrote out two such checks to Geller. By last year, most of the forty grand was gone."

"Any indication that anyone tried to stop her, or helped her take care of her money?"

"None."

"What about her other expenses? Did they go up, down, anything?"

"Down. Way down. By the end, she was doing little but paying bills and seeing Geller. Even her grocery bills went really low, as if she couldn't have been eating much or eating right."

"I can't get over the fact that nobody seemed

to care," Richie said. "No one tried to stop her or help her."

"Well, that's where it got really odd," Shay said. "Somebody did. Sandy Geller. After most of her own money was gone, he started sending her five-hundred dollars a month. It was the difference between her having to leave her apartment and being able to cover her basic expenses."

Richie nodded. "I've heard that before about him. I don't get it. First, he gladly took a grand a month from a little old lady, and then the pillar of society gave her back five hundred? That bastard is all heart, isn't he?"

"How many con men pay their marks back anything?" Shay asked.

"Good question." Richie rubbed his temples. "Damn, but it just doesn't make sense. Is it that he's got a conscience after all? Didn't want to see her thrown out on the street? Or are we missing something? Actually, if she was thrown out, the city's social services or somebody might have questioned where her money went. And if she told them, they might have come down on Geller like flies on shit, which is exactly what he is."

"There's more to it than that." Shay looked like the cat that swallowed the canary.

This, Richie knew, was the money shot—the part of the story Shay had been itching to tell. "Shoot," he said.

"I was so curious about Geller, I hacked into his bank accounts. The guy's loaded; close to seven million in Swiss banks. But it wasn't until I looked at the money in this country, the three or so million he leaves here, that things got really interesting."

"Okay."

"He's sending monthly payments to eight *other* people—both men and women—who at one time had sent money, tens of thousands of dollars in every case, to him."

That was the last thing Richie was expecting to hear. "Eight? What is he, some friggin' Robin Hood?"

"One lives in Denver where Geller was located before he went to Los Angeles, two in LA, and the rest in San Francisco."

Richie just shook his head.

"And one of the women who's been paying him quite a bit of money recently is your mother's friend Geri."

"So I've heard," Richie said glumly.

Then Shay's voice turned low and quiet as he added, "Your mother's now seeing him, too. To the tune last month of one thousand dollars."

Richie's mouth dropped open. "Christ almighty!"

oOo

"Richie, what's wrong with you? You aren't yourself."

Richie had been so horrified by Shay's news, he drove straight to his mother's home. She lived on the top floor of a three-story building on Russian Hill. Richie had bought the building for her a few years earlier. She rented out the flat below her and also rented the garage since she didn't drive.

Judging from the way his mother was studying him, coming here might have been a mistake. Carmela was in her early sixties, short, and a little overweight. Richie guessed she was still considered attractive because when men around her age saw her, they inevitably stood a little taller and sucked in their gut—not that he didn't find it kind of gross to think of anyone checking out his mother.

"There's nothing wrong," he said. He couldn't just start questioning her about what she and Geri were up to. Her hackles would rise and he'd get nowhere. Instead, he had to ease into the conversation, slowly.

They were sitting at the kitchen table. Although the kitchen had state-of-the-art appliances and new cream-colored cabinetry, it still had a cozy, old-fashioned look. Carmela poured them each a cup of coffee and then put a plate of home-made cookies within Richie's easy reach.

"You want some lunch?" She opened the refrigerator to see what she could offer him.

"No."

"See, I told you." Carmela shut the refrigerator door and then stared at him as if she were considering calling a priest to give him last rites.

"I've got to watch my weight," he said gently. "It goes on too easy."

She sat across the table from him. "It's the age. You're getting up there, Richie." She added a half-teaspoon of sugar to her coffee and stirred it. "You got to get married before you get fat and lose your hair. I hope you take after your father's side. They all had such hair, wavy, like yours is now. On my side, the men all look like cue balls by the time they're fifty."

"I'm not getting married because I might lose my hair."

"You're too old to mess around."

"What's all this about my age?" he cried.

"You heard me. You think I don't know why you're not eating?" She had dark brown eyes, and short copper-colored hair that was styled every week and then so heavily sprayed it didn't move a single strand until she went back to the hairdresser. Right now, her eyes turned beady as they bored into him.

"Because I'm not hungry?"

"Because you're still thinking too much about *her.*"

"Her?"

"The cop! Who else?"

"Christ, Ma! I'm not thinking about anybody. Give me a break!"

"I can see it." She stared at him hard. "These are a mother's eyes. They know when her son is getting ready to have his heart ripped out and torn into little pieces."

"My heart's just fine."

"She got you shot!" Carmela waggled her forefinger at him. "Don't you forget it!"

"She did no such thing." He shoved aside the coffee as if about to leave. "Ma, I can't take this!"

She stood and put her hand on his shoulder, stopping him. "You'll be happier if you're married, Richie, to some sweet girl."

"I'm happy now," he bellowed, then slumped back in his seat. She sat down again. "Besides," he added, "before I get married, I do want to be in love—at least a little."

"Love? You've had love. True love. May Isabella rest in peace." Carmela quickly crossed herself. "Now, you just need security."

"Don't talk about Isabella, okay?"

Carmela folded her arms. "Look, Dora Petalucchio's daughter just broke off her engagement because her father caught her fiancé with another woman." She nodded the way she always did when she had a good story to tell. "Not just with her, but *with* her, if you know what I'm saying—in the men's room at the Sons of Italy hall, no less. They thought no one would try to use a stall, only the urinals, but her old man ate a bad *cannoli* and what're you gonna do? Anyway, the daughter, Kathy, Kaylie—one of those American 'k' names—is already thirty. So she doesn't have time to start over—to go out and date and do all that stuff to find someone to love. But she'd make a good wife for you."

"I heard about that," Richie admitted. "But I'm not taking Joey Hands' cast off."

"Joey Hands? I thought he was Italian?"

"He was. Is. The guys call him that because he's … Just forget it, Ma. Believe me, if she's not attractive enough for Joey Hands to marry, forget it."

"But you need—"

"No. I don't." He stood. "I'm leaving, and when you want to have a normal conversation about séances and ghosts, you call me."

The reference to Sandy Geller didn't faze her. He headed for the door with Carmela following, her words ringing in his ears. "I'll say no more, Richie. But I want you to be happy; right now, you're a mess. I pray so much for you, my knees are getting blisters!"

Chapter 8

Rebecca sat alone back at her desk and fumed.

Mr. Stick-Up-His-Butt FBI Agent had told her that Richie was a fixer. She knew what a "fixer" was, although there were fixers … and then there were *fixers*. Most of the time, it meant someone who could mend a bad situation for a client, someone who knew their way around the law, or the system, or enough important people to get a client out of a jam, legal or otherwise.

She understood, now, exactly why Richie didn't broadcast his job.

Was she surprised when Agent Seymour had told her that? She had to admit, she'd suspected it. Richie knew too many important people and had too many people reporting to him about topics of the hush-hush variety. Did it mean he was a criminal? No, but it could mean he was walking a fine line. When a person helps enough big shots with money and influence, soon, that person learns enough secrets that he ends up with money and influence as well. That's when it's easy to cross over to the dark side.

She was going to have to find out if he had or not. No more coyness; no more hints. He needed to be straight with her.

Richie weighed heavy on her mind when she met with Sandy Geller. Geller picked her up outside Homicide in a Mercedes two-seat roadster.

"I hope we didn't have too much demon talk last night," he said with a sly grin.

"No. Not at all. Actually, I'd like to hear more about demons."

"I should think there are a lot of them in your line of work."

"Perhaps too many," she murmured as she forced her thoughts away from Richie to study Sandy a moment. His light brown hair was naturally lank, and without mascara and other make-up his eyes were faint. His nose was straight and small, and his lips cupid-bow shaped, which she never particularly liked on a man. "I take it you believe in demons."

Sandy's lips upturned. "Some people are good, some are bad. Why should spirits be any different?

Demons are simply spirits who want to do us harm. And yes, they do exist. A lot of mediums will go into a trance state and allow a spirit to take over control of his or her body. I don't do that because it can lead to permanent possession by demonic forces."

"Oh? I thought mediums were supposed to allow spirits to take over their bodies," Rebecca said. "Isn't that what you do in your show?"

He smiled stiffly. "It's not exactly a 'show.' And I *channel* the spirit, not let it take over."

"What about the kind of séance where the medium asks the spirit to do strange things like blow out candles and ring bells?"

"Ah, yes!" he said. "It's actually quite interesting. That type of séance became wildly popular in the mid-eighteen hundreds, because of an incident that took place near Rochester, New York," Sandy said with a smile.

"Really?"

"Oh, yes, the infamous Fox sisters. Maggie and Kate Fox were only fifteen and eleven years old when they claimed to have made contact with the spirit of a murdered peddler."

Sandy proceeded to tell her the story of the Fox family and how unexplained noises began to afflict the family home. At some point, the younger girl, Kate, started asking whoever was making the noise some questions. The questions soon led to a system using a number of raps as an answer. From the answers, the family realized the dead peddler was the one causing the noises.

"Neighbors were brought in to see what was happening," Sandy said, "and the girls became famous practically overnight. Soon, people rushed to the Fox house to watch the girls interact with the spirit. The girls soon began conducting séances with their older sister, Leah, working as their manager."

"So it was a scam from the beginning," Rebecca said.

"We don't know that," Sandy offered. "But we do know that as the girls' fame and popularity grew, so did skepticism. They were accused of tricks, including concealing of lead balls beneath their dresses to make noise. People formed committees to test them, but couldn't find any evidence of fraud. Things changed for the better after the girls held a séance for the famous author James Fenimore Cooper. He came away convinced of their authenticity and wrote news articles about his experience with them. Those writings help spread their fame.

"By the 1850's, you could find spiritualist groups in many major American cities, as well as England and Europe. But soon, mediums vied with each other for attention, and did increasingly outrageous stunts to entertain their audiences. Levitation was a huge one. Such things pushed the 'Rochester Rappers' as the Fox sisters were known, out of the spotlight. In fact, the girls tried to recant and regain popularity by saying they had been instructed by their older sister on how to fake their connections with the dead, but few people cared about them at that point. Eventually, both died as penniless alcoholics."

"What a story," Rebecca said, surprised she had never heard it before.

Sandy nodded. "It is, and it's also what gives psychics a bad name. Tables levitating, pendulums swinging, candles going out or coming on all by themselves, automatic writing, Ouija boards, planchettes—they're all easily faked. It's ludicrous for anyone to ask a spirit to answer questions with a 'rap once for yes, twice for no.' Do people really think spirits are here to play a game of twenty questions?"

oOo

Richie wanted nothing as much as to meet Rebecca after her work day ended and to talk to her. He managed to convince himself he'd been wrong about her reasons for spending last evening with Sandy Geller. She couldn't possibly have any romantic interest in the guy. It was intellectual, that's all. And she was investigating.

He hoped.

But before he could contact Rebecca, Claire Baxter had contacted him. She was scared and said she needed to see him right away. He believed she was innocent of the FBI's accusation that she consorted with known smugglers of stolen Middle Eastern artifacts. He drove over to her condo near the crest of Nob Hill.

Her front door was at ground level, and stairs led up to her living area which was a testament to her success. Filled with paintings, sculptures, and antique furniture, it was beautiful. Even the clocks on her walls were works of art. When he reached the top of the staircase, he gawked at her in shock.

One side of her face was swollen and bruised. Her wrists were also black and blue, and her usually perfect manicure had several "fake" fingernails missing. She had clearly been crying. As he studied her, she threw her arms around him.

"What happened?" he asked, holding her. She was in her fifties, although no one would ever know it by looking at her. She had a great figure, and usually hid any wrinkles she might have had with Botox, a hairstyle of thick bangs down to her eyelashes, turtlenecks and neck scarves. Right now, though, she looked her age and more.

"Those men, those horrible men!" She began to sob.

He guided her to the living room. Chairs had been knocked over. He lifted two spindly ones, but after looking at them, decided they'd better sit on the small chaise lounge. The antique furniture filling her house might be pricey, but it was also stiff, undersized, and uncomfortable. Once they were settled, he said, "Now, tell me what happened."

"Two men were in my house when I got home. They're going to kill me." Her hands shook as she grabbed his lapels. "You've got to get me a new identity. I need to run."

"Why would they want to kill you?"

"Because the FBI came back here again—to my house! Those men said if I tell the FBI who they are …" She started breathing too hard to speak.

"But the FBI has no proof that you have the Nimrud gold jewelry, right? Only hearsay that you were selling some of it?"

She swallowed hard. "They somehow found out that I had three pieces here."

Now it was his turn to stop breathing. She had lied to him, swearing she had nothing to do with any jewelry that even resembled the Nimrud gold. "You had smuggled artifacts here?"

"I didn't know they were contraband. Only that they were Middle Eastern and old and valuable. I had to have them to show my buyers. No sight-unseen sales—ever—in antiquities. But now"—she burst into more tears—"the FBI confiscated them and told me to either give them the name of the seller or go to jail. That horrible Agent Seymour claims he's watching me constantly."

Richie ran his fingers through his hair. So now, by showing up here, he would also be on the FBI's radar—if he wasn't already simply because of associating with her. This was getting better by the minute. "Let's think about this. If the FBI is watching, they must have seen the two men who attacked you."

She shook her head. "Maybe not. They disarmed my alarm system from the back door and used it to come in and to leave. I doubt the FBI is out there."

"But aren't all those back yards small with no street access? How could they get out?"

"Who knows?" She shrugged.

He took a deep breath. He really hated this kind of garbage. "Did they say anything else?"

"They sure did. They want their money. The three pieces the FBI took are worth a hundred-fifty thousand dollars. They want that much from me. And if they don't get it, I'm dead. I don't have that much cash. I've got to run."

"What about your art pieces? Do you have any that are worth that kind of money?"

"Sure, but it takes time to sell valuable art and antiquities, Richie."

"Look, come up with at least two-hundred grand worth of whatever antiquities and art that you can, plus appraisals to prove the value. Tell me how to reach the people you're dealing with and I'll see if legitimate artifacts will interest them enough to leave you alone. Sound good?"

"Two hundred grand?" she asked, incredulously.

"You need to convince them to take the deal. Less than two hundred would be an insult. Or would you prefer they kill you and steal everything you own? You said they've broken in here once already, right?"

Her tears again overflowed and once more she wrapped her arms around him. "Can you lend me some money Richie?"

"Not on your life."

She drew back, pouting. "By the way, when the FBI was questioning me, I said you could vouch for my story that the art dealers I'm working with have reputations for dealing with legitimate merchandise—as do I."

He felt as if his hair was on fire. "You know that's not true," he shouted. "I warned you—"

"So what," she yelled back. "I need help! Your help!"

Richie was beyond furious at her. "Get the piece you want to give the Iraqis, the paperwork, and let me know how to contact them. I'll handle it. And stop your goddamn talking to the FBI."

Chapter 9

Half Moon Bay was on the ocean a half-hour or so south of San Francisco, but it could have been on a different planet. The small coastal town seemed to be a forgotten throwback to the mid-twentieth century.

Sandy drove three miles past the town center and then turned down a road heading westward towards a small peninsula. The road ended at a padlocked wrought-iron fence. He had the key.

The estate was twenty acres in size, and Rebecca was surprised at how far Sandy drove along the private road before she saw, atop a rise, a two-story white clapboard farmhouse facing the ocean. The parking area was on lower land on the house's south side.

After parking, they walked up a narrow footpath to the front door. Sandy unlocked it and disarmed the security system. "I'm paying for access to this house to do a TV special. The owner won't sell, sure that the more publicity the place gets, the more valuable it'll become. I don't know about that, but I do know it's haunted."

He gave her a quick tour. A parlor, dining room, kitchen, and pantry were on the first floor, and three bedrooms and a bathroom on the second. The rooms were quite small, but charmingly decorated and furnished with antiques. Old family portraits lined the walls. Sandy explained that every so often the owner opened it up for the public, charging twenty dollars each for the opportunity. Only by having it furnished to look the way it did back in the 1920's when the tragedy occurred was he able to make his visitors happy.

They might not see the ghost, but they could see how she lived, ate, and slept.

"I'm still waiting to hear the ghost's story," Rebecca said.

Sandy didn't get a chance to relate it because just then the photographer and a make-up artist arrived. Rebecca found it interesting to watch the photographer and Sandy work. Sandy wore one of the same romantic-looking shirts as at his performance, and the make-up artist fluffed his long hair and then applied a blend of dark creams and eye make-up so that his cheeks appeared more hollow, and his eyes larger and deeper set than they were on their own.

The photographer and Sandy worked with the home's lighting and used old clothes to give a sense that a woman who wore dark Victorian clothing was lurking just beyond the shadows. At one point, Sandy put a dress on a hanger and attached it to a light fixture dangling from the ceiling. He turned off most of the lights and then had the photographer take the picture through a mirror. The light from the flash against the mirror blurred out almost everything except the nearly black dress. It looked as if it were being worn by a woman floating across the room.

An hour or so later, when the shoot was done and the photographer and make-up artist had departed, Sandy showed Rebecca a Coleman cooler containing a bottle of blush wine and half a dozen sandwiches neatly bundled in Saran Wrap.

"Want to have a picnic on the beach?" he said.

Rebecca smiled. "Only if you promise to finally tell me the ghost's back story." She realized that she had chosen her words carefully. Somehow saying it like that didn't admit to the idea that she might actually believe that this house was haunted.

"Ah," he said. "That's a tale that needs much strong wine to hear."

The land on which the house sat was like a finger jutting into the ocean. On its south side, cliffs dropped sharply down to rough, rock-laden water, with scarcely any beach available. North of the house, however, the landscape was much less steep and rugged. There, Sandy led her to an easy-to-traverse path down to the beach.

As they sat and spread out the light feast—the wine and the sandwiches had remained nicely chilled in the cooler—Rebecca remembered how much she had always loved the smell of sand and sea. She couldn't resist digging her fingers into the dry sand and watching it slide through as she pulled her hand back up. The waves were high and crashed loudly on the shore, and a chilly sea breeze nipped at her face. She zipped up her leather jacket.

As they ate, Sandy told the tale of the ghost of Falls Meadow—the name given to the land back in the days when a creek ran through the property and created a small waterfall that dropped down to a lovely well-tended meadow.

oOo

Wilhelm Bruckman left Germany in 1849 when he heard about the California gold rush. He was one of the lucky ones. Not only did he find gold, he had the sense not to spend it on high living.

Instead, he bought a large piece of property on the coast south of San Francisco, as well as a number of dairy cows and a bull to support himself the way his family had done in Germany. He built a home and eventually sent for a German woman to became his wife.

Only one son, Johan, survived to adulthood. When Wilhelm was dying, he told Johan where on the property he had hidden his remaining gold, but warned him to never use it unless absolutely necessary.

By 1925, Johan, by then an old man and a widower, lived on the property with his son, Gunter, the son's wife, Astrid, and their young daughter, Inga. Their dairy business supported the family, and at times to augment their income, Gunter would do some bass fishing in the Pacific.

They lived well, secure in the fact that if anything happened, they had Wilhelm's gold to fall back on. But things were not happy in the house. Gunter was restless, and unhappy living on a dreary, remote peninsula and working the land the way his father and grandfather had done. He wanted more from life.

His wife, Astrid, discovered that he had been cheating on her with a woman from the town. In revenge, she cut through a plank in the bottom of the small skiff he used when fishing.

She didn't cut through it all the way, but only far enough so that, as the boat continued farther out over the ocean, pressure on its wooden underside would tear the plank apart. Water would flood the boat and sink it. She was sure Gunter would survive the dunking being a strong swimmer, and there were always a number of other fishing boats out on the water. She also believed that, although he wouldn't be able to prove anything, in his heart he'd know she was behind his close call. He would spend the rest of his days looking over his shoulder at her.

One winter's day as she was shopping in town,

she heard that the bass were running close and many of the men were heading out to fish. She felt certain Gunter would join them. She smiled and went about her shopping.

Before she knew it, a thick gray wall of fog had blown in off the ocean, turning the sky dark. She couldn't help but wonder if her husband might be hidden by the fog when his skiff took on water.

She thought of finding someone on the pier to go out and tell Gunter that his father believed something might be wrong with the skiff, and he shouldn't take it out that day.

But then, she saw the "other woman" walking along the sidewalk, and her heart hardened. She went into a cafe where she dawdled over tea and a sandwich.

Eventually, with the fog so heavy she could scarcely see her hand in front of her face, she headed for home. There, she saw old Johan, but not her daughter.

The old man told her that Gunter had taken Inga with him earlier that day, and they hadn't yet returned.

She ran from the house.

They said you could hear her calling her husband and daughter's names as she ran along the pier. The fog hung low on the bay, and nothing could be seen out on the water.

She begged others to search for them, that she believed something might be wrong—a feeling—but no one dared go out in the thick pea soup fog until Gunter and Inga were long overdue.

Neither Gunter, Inga, or the boat were ever seen again.

The townspeople say that Astrid was so distraught and guild-ridden, she confessed to Johan all that she had done. He went to the police, insisting that they arrest her and hang her for murder.

But they had no bodies, no case, and apparently some sightings convinced them that Gunter had sunk or otherwise destroyed the boat, took his daughter, and left the area.

Johan became so furious at them, he had a heart-attack. He died cursing Astrid and saying she would have no peace for all eternity.

She spent the rest of her life half-insane, walking around the house, going from window to window to look out at the ocean. The locals say she's continued to do that even after death, and that she forces anyone who attempts to live in the house out of it as she waits for Gunter and Inga to return.

oOo

Rebecca, ever the cynic, wondered how much of the story was true. She'd heard similar ones over the years involving different times and different places. But as she looked up at the house from the beach, the curtain over an upper-story window moved, revealing something dark just beyond it. She stared, but then the curtain went back to its original position.

"Is someone in the house?" she asked.

"No. Why?" Sandy turned to face the building. *"Don't tell me you saw something?"*

"No, not at all. Maybe a draft. That's all."

"There's no draft. My God! We've got to try to conjure her up. Let's go back to the house." Sandy looked more like a big, enthusiastic puppy than a serious psychic.

"I don't think so," she said with a laugh.

He cocked his head. "Well, if you want to be practical about it, we can call her to us in order to ask her where the old German's gold is hidden."

"You think it's still here?"

"Frankly, I think it was a made-up story to add more interest to the place. And to give people a better reason for coming all the way out here than simply to see a ghost."

She chuckled. "That's remarkably cynical for a psychic medium."

"Maybe I think ghosts are a better class of people than the living." He smiled just enough to deepen his dimples. "Come on. Let's go. It's freezing out here."

"No. I'm enjoying the beach."

"Ah ha! You do believe!"

"I do not!"

"Prove it." He held out his hand to hers and waited.

"Oh, for Pete's sake!" Feeling irritated, but also nervous—had she seen anything, or was it just the play of light and shadow bouncing off the ocean in the twilight?—she put her hand in his. He helped her to her feet, and they went back up the hill.

From the rise, Rebeca saw a wall of fog out on

the ocean, heading inland, reminding her of the ghost's story and of fog blanketing the area and leading to the tragedy. A foghorn made a baleful cry, sending shivers down her spine as she followed Sandy into the house.

The house had turned icy cold. He turned on the lights in the dining room, but they had little power, leaving them and the chairs and table in dim shadows. She suddenly didn't want to be here, but felt as if she were intruding on someone, or something.

Sandy lit a candle on the table and then shut the electric lights. "Let's sit at the table," he said. He and Rebecca faced each other, the candle between them as they reached across the table and held hands, one hand on each side of the candle. "Now, I want you to look at the flickering candlelight, and clear your mind. We both need to relax and then open our minds to the presence in this house."

"I thought you said that could be dangerous," she said.

"Only for a novice." His voice was filled with pride. "I know what I'm doing."

"Look at the candle, Rebecca," he said. "Concentrate only on the flame and the sound of my voice." He began to breathe deeply and to go through a series of relaxing words about each limb of her body growing heavy and relaxing until she felt at one with the candle, its flame, and even the house.

She tried to keep a smile on her face to show how silly she felt doing this, but something about his voice made her start to believe that to relax was very good, even desirable. Her eyes grew so heavy she needed to shut them. Her breathing slowed.

He talked to her for a while before he asked her to open her eyes and look around the room. "This room and the kitchen were where Astrid spent most of her time. What do you see?"

She stared a long time. "I think … Is that a shadow in the kitchen doorway?"

"Is it? You tell me."

"No. It's nothing. There's only darkness now."

"Do you see a woman? Perhaps she has blond hair, parted in the middle and pulled back? Her dress is most likely black with a high collar that fits tight around her neck."

"I can't tell. I don't think I see anything at all. I don't like this."

"Relax, Rebecca. It's fine. I'm guiding you."

"I feel so sad."

"That's Astrid," he said softly. "She has the sorrow of a woman who knows she's killed the only ones she's ever loved. She was a wife and a mother. Have you ever been a wife or mother?"

"No."

"Your mother—is she still alive?"

"Yes."

"Do you see her often?"

"Very little."

"Why?"

"She's far away. I disappoint her."

"Why? What terrible thing did you do, Rebecca? You can tell me."

"Nothing. My sister is prettier, and very ladylike. She's in Hollywood because she wants to become an actress. I'm not ladylike at all."

"Your father—is he dead?"

"Yes."

"What's his name?"

"Benjamin."

"Called …?"

"Ben."

"Did Ben love you, Rebecca?"

"Yes, but he was always working, so I didn't see him very often."

"Tell me how he died?"

"His heart. I don't like to think about him. I couldn't bear it when he died."

"Tell me more about—"

"No!" Her breath caught.

"What?" he asked. "Rebecca?"

"There. In the mirror!" She stood and so did he. He let go of her hands as he spun around to look in the mirror over the sideboard behind him.

Rebecca looked around. She found herself standing, facing a mirror. Sandy, too, was looking at it, his face white, his eyes frightened. She glanced down at the candle. It was considerably lower than when she last remembered looking at it. "What happened?" she asked.

He spun towards her. "Are you all right?" he asked.

"I'm so sorry! Did I fall asleep? Why are we standing here?"

"I believe you nodded off and then had a nightmare. You suddenly stood up. So much for my charm," he said with a small laugh. "Time to head back to the city, I'd say. But now that you've seen all this, please tell me you'll come to a séance at my office tomorrow night. I promise you, you will not fall asleep."

Rebecca felt strange. Had she really fallen asleep so easily? That wasn't like her. He mentioned a nightmare, but a person usually remembers nightmares, and she remembered nothing. She looked around and a felt a sudden chill, the sort her mother used to say meant someone was walking over your grave.

"I can't believe I fell asleep," she said.

He chuckled nervously. "Probably too much sea air. You may have caught a chill. Anyway, yesterday you asked about the Sandoristas," he said. "Well, the séance will be an opportunity to meet some of them. Say you'll attend. You'll be my guest."

Sandoristas … yes, of course. "I'll be there," she said.

"One more thing. Do you"—he swallowed

hard—"do you now see anything in the kitchen, or perhaps in the mirror?"

"In the mirror?" Whatever was he talking about she wondered. Yet, as she looked at it, she felt that, if she could take a cloth and rub the mirror hard—as if cleaning a window—she might clear the way through the mirror and see …

"No," she said quickly. "I see nothing at all."

oOo

Richie finally got away from Claire Baxter, and once in his car, tried to reach Rebecca by phone. She didn't answer, which wasn't unusual when she was working. He drove to Homicide. Her SUV was in the parking lot so he went up to see her. Calderon and Benson were there working a murder-suicide. From them, he learned Rebecca had actually left work early that day.

That was a puzzle. She never left early.

More of a puzzle was her SUV—leaving it meant someone had picked her up there at work. But who?

He tried again to reach her by phone. Same lousy results.

Some months back when he first met her and

thought she'd be an interesting date, she often ignored his calls. He couldn't say he blamed her. So, he got over it. Mostly, he got over *her*. Or so he thought. But then, things got complicated.

He called a guy he knew in the SFPD's Civic Center precinct where Rebecca's latest boyfriend worked and asked if Ray Torres was on the job that night. He learned Torres was cruising around in his patrol car at that very moment, his partner by his side.

For some reason, her dating Torres didn't bother him—or, not a whole lot, at least. But the thought of her with that psychic …

Could she be with Geller again tonight? Was she getting to like him? Or maybe feeling something even more serious?

Chapter 10

In Homicide the next morning, Rebecca was surprised to learn Richie had shown up the prior evening looking for her. Since he left no message, she assumed he must have wanted an update on her investigation. She had nothing to tell him, and no time for him today, in any case. She would be spending a good chunk of the day in court waiting to testify. She was almost glad of that because, when she did see Richie-the-fixer, she had questions for him which could lead to some unpleasant answers.

When she got back to her desk in late afternoon, she found a half dozen messages from Agent Seymour. All he wanted was to know if she'd contacted Richie and if she'd learned anything about Claire Baxter. She told him she'd get back to him if or when either happened.

By the time evening came, she was almost glad to spend it watching Sandy conduct a séance. At least the dead weren't "fixers" hanging around her office uninvited, or snoops calling her phone multiple times.

She headed for Sandy's offices. His assistant, Lucian, met her at the door and led her into the large room she had noticed two days earlier. It was now a very different space. The sofa and lamps had been moved to the walls, and center stage was a large round table. The room was lit only by candlelight, and the drapes had been shut so no glaring city lights shone in.

She thought she would be early for the séance, but a number of people were already present. She walked in and looked around, but didn't see Sandy anywhere. Lucian, too, had disappeared. Back to man the door, she supposed. Three women and two men were in the room. She was the youngest by a good thirty years, she suspected, but they looked like a well-heeled group, with expensive albeit casual clothes, shoes, and stylish jewelry. At the same time, they all looked a bit wide eyed and strained, as if waiting or hoping for something.

"Hello," the oldest fellow walked up to her. "You must be a newcomer. I'd have noticed you before, that's for sure." He winked. "Donald Luff's the name. Some like to call me 'the Luff Bug.'"

She didn't know whether to laugh or if he was actually being serious. He looked to be in his seventies, about 5'7" or so, and wiry, wearing a suit with a pocket handkerchief that matched his tie.

"Rebecca Mayfield," she said, "and I am new. Have you been coming here long?"

He explained that he started attending séances a few years earlier because he missed his wife, and then quickly learned that he had an ability to conjure spirits. He had been a computer mainframe programmer "in his youth," and although he switched over to programming PCs, he simply didn't enjoy it the way he had the big boxes. Now, as a Sandorista, he liked to say he went "from high-tech to no-tech."

"So you're a Sandorista," she said, doing her best to sound impressed. What luck, she thought, to have found one so easily. "I've heard of them."

Donald Luff beamed. "Yes, I am. There are four of us here tonight, in fact. Myself, Candace Carter, and Henry and Marta Highfield—the couple over by the wine. All of us love coming and do so as often as allowed."

"Allowed?" Rebecca asked.

"Sandy only has room for so many people at a séance. They can't be too large, you know. So you have to apply, and then he makes his selection, attempting to have a mix of men and women, experienced and newcomers, and so on. Since there aren't that many men involved, I'm able to attend pretty often, same as Henry Highfield. For me, it's also a nice way to meet some pretty neat gals, if you know what I mean." He chuckled.

She really couldn't take much more of this character. "I'd love to meet the Highfields," she said.

"I'll introduce you." The eager beaver took her arm, led her across the room, and made introductions.

She quickly learned that Marta and Henry Highfield had been followers of Sandor Geller ever since attending one of his events when they were vacationing in Denver, some fifteen years earlier. They were in their sixties and had been married for over thirty years, having spent many of those years studying psychics and mediums. Henry, with thick white hair, a rangy build, and dark tan, had taught high school math and science before retiring, and Marta had been a paralegal at a law firm. Marta was still attractive with dyed blond hair, and what was probably a once voluptuous figure that had now thickened with age. The couple confessed to Rebecca that they had "dabbled" with becoming mediums themselves, but found it too scary when they had felt something demonic coming closer to them. After that, they decided to let Sandy be their go-between with "the other side."

Rebecca was finding this almost too easy. Usually, it was like pulling teeth to get people she came into contact with to talk about themselves and their interests. These people all but spewed out their stories for her. Almost as if concentrating so much on the dead made them value their time with someone alive more than most people did.

The thought jarred her. It was, she hated to admit it, rather like the life of a homicide detective. She pushed aside the thought. "So, tell me," she said to Marta, "do you come to these séances very often?"

"Absolutely!" Marta exclaimed. "We were so thrilled when Sandy moved his home and offices to

San Francisco some five years earlier, we could scarcely stand it. Sandy's wonderful, and because we've followed him for so long, he only charges us the one participant price, although the two of us attend. Isn't that wonderful and generous of him?"

Rebecca thought quickly. "I'm here as a guest tonight. If I did come on my own, could you tell me the cost to take part in a séance?"

"It's five hundred dollars," Henry said. "And worth every penny. It's not often you get a vision of the life to come. Most people sit around and play the agnostic, saying they don't know if there's life after death. Or they want proof. Well, it's right here. All the proof they could want. They're just too damned stupid or lazy to come and see for themselves."

"Now, Henry," Marta said with a smile, "don't be harsh. Not everyone is open to reality."

Rebecca was struck momentarily speechless by not only the amount of money these people were paying for a couple of hours with Sandy, but that they were so completely convinced what happened at the séances was real. She noticed that Donald Luff had left her side and was now talking to two woman who had entered after she had. One of them appeared quite young and wore jeans and a leather jacket while the other looked middle-aged with graying hair and glasses.

"If you'll excuse me, I'm going to introduce myself to the other Sandorista here," Rebecca said to Henry and Marta. "I really enjoy talking to people who have some experience with all this. It was nice meeting you."

"We'll talk again, I'm sure," Marta said.

Rebecca found Candace Carter, who stood alone after wandering over to a trash bin to throw away her plastic water glass. Candace appeared to be another strong, spry septuagenarian. Her short hair was dyed brown, her make-up light, and she wore a bright green pants suit.

"Excuse me," Rebecca said, then introduced herself as a person interested in learning more about the afterlife.

"You've come to the right place." Candace smiled pleasantly at her and then looked over the room. "I think you'll enjoy it here. I do. It's my way of being around people I like."

"The Sandoristas?" Rebecca asked.

"Hell, no." She chuckled. "I mean my friends who have died."

Rebecca gaped.

"I hardly knew what to do with myself after I retired," Candace began. She had taught second graders until she was forced to retire at age 70. She confessed that before she found Sandy and the Sandoristas, she had been lost.

"Rebecca, I'm so glad you decided to join us," a familiar male voice said.

Rebecca turned to see Sandy approach. As opposed to the older group who had dressed up a bit, he wore jeans and a bulky off-white fisherman's knit sweater. He greeted Candace quickly, then faced Rebecca again. "You seem to be making friends."

"Yes. I'm meeting very interesting and nice people," she said with a smile at Candace who all but had stars in her eyes as she looked at Sandy. School girls swooning over pop idols had nothing on her.

"Excellent! Well, now that I'm here, it's time to get started," Sandy said.

He began by having them all sit at the table.

Rebecca found herself between Donald Luff and Marta Highfield. She noticed that the four Sandoristas present had automatically positioned themselves between the four newcomers.

"Before we start," Sandy said, "I want to explain a couple of things to our new people. First, forget everything you've ever heard or seen on TV or in the movies about séances. They're all crap."

Everyone laughed.

"Here, we rely on science. Okay, I can feel you newcomers laughing again." Sandy's dimples deepening as he smiled and went around the table, catching each woman's eye and holding it a moment, causing a spate of more nervous laughter. "Let me put you at ease by letting you in on a secret. Beginning in the 1970's, the CIA spent billions of dollars studying psychic phenomena, which led to its Stargate project on psychic remote viewing. In it, people used their brain power to psychically view what someone else—perhaps on the other side of the world—was seeing at that very moment. And, here's the secret: it worked. It wasn't stopped until the 1990's, not because it wasn't producing results—FOIA requests have shown some very real results—but because politicians grew tired of being mocked by their constituents for throwing money away on 'charlatans.' But I know, just as the CIA does, and now you also know, this is *not* trickery."

The Sandoristas nodded sagely. Donald Luff caught Rebecca's eye and winked. She ignored the old fart. He really thought he was something.

"So, you may be thinking, what is it? Those of us in what some call the 'New Age' understand that we all have a Spirit Self, and that self is aided through life by our Spirit Guide. When you die, that connection does not end, which means all of us have the ability to communicate psychically. We can contact each other through channeling, remote viewing and other such means, or with the dead through Spirit Guides.

"The only danger," he continued, "is for the medium. We mediums know that when we open ourselves up to The Other, we are open. Period. That means anything can enter—*anything*. And when you've experienced what I have, you know this is dangerous. That's why anyone who is a serious psychic does not, I repeat, *does not* encourage a layman who hasn't had a lot of training to try to do this on her own."

Of course not, Rebecca thought. If he or she succeeded, Sandy wouldn't get paid. This was getting tiresome, and she was sure wasn't any help in determining what might have happened to Neda Fourman and Betty Faroni.

"Are you ready to begin?"

Everyone murmured "yes." He asked them to hold hands, and to rest their hands on the tabletop. "I will now ask my assistant to blow out all candles except the one on the table."

Rebecca was startled when a man, dressed all in black, stepped out from the shadows with a candle snuffer. It was his assistant, Lucian.

Donald Luff squeezed her hand and then rubbed her knuckles with his thumb. She wasn't amused and simply tightened her hand on his. A lot. His eyes widened, and then his mouth opened. She pretty much figured how much pressure to put on before he'd let out a yelp, and she eased up before that point. He stared at her, red-faced, and with a little tear in the corner of one eye.

She focused on Sandy.

"For the newcomers," Sandy said, "my friend, Lucian, will sit quietly in the corner and be ready to assist if any of you faints or feels as if a spirit is trying to take over your body or your mind. These things have happened, so it is always wise to have an observer who can step in. Sometimes you might be so completely overwhelmed by a spirit that you don't even know you're in trouble. Lucian will be watching for those circumstances as well."

Rebecca imagined the other newcomers would be frightened by such words, and she was right. It put into their heads the possibility they would do and say things they normally wouldn't. The power of suggestion, she imagined, could create some interesting results.

The room was now almost completely dark except for the candle on the table. Its shape was low and squat, and as Sandy pulled it closer to him, its light reflected upward on his face making him look positively demonic. Once again, Rebecca found herself on the verge of snorting with derision. She and her sister had done the same thing with candles when they were kids, seeing who would make the scariest "demon."

"Now," Sandy said, "I need all of you to focus your thoughts on what we are about to do."

He began with long breaths in and out, getting everyone to breathe in unison. Next, he went to the typical calming exercises of "You're getting sleepy" and "Your head is getting heavy." Instead of concentrating on what he was saying, Rebecca paid more attention on the others, keeping her eyes open and watching. She couldn't help but wonder why she'd fallen asleep so easily the night before. It wasn't like her to be such a limp noodle. She had seen this sort of thing in connection with hypnosis, but she wasn't a person who could be hypnotized in any way, shape or form. She would never give any other person that much power over her.

Sandy began a call for spirits. He spoke in little more than a whisper, calm, and inviting. "Come to us, spirit. Talk with us. We're here because we want to communicate with you. We want to know you, and to let you know you are not forgotten."

The ensuing silence was unnerving and Rebecca was beginning to feel she was wasting her time. She had an idea of getting up and walking out. Then Sandy let out a hushed whisper. "I feel a presence," he said.

Marta's hand tightened on Rebecca's fingers. Nervous energy filled the room.

"Are you someone that we know?" Sandy asked.

Everyone waited in silence.

"The spirit is very faint," Sandy murmured. "Almost too … wait. I can feel it. It's trying to reach out to us. Ah! Donald. It's a woman. She's saying 'Donald.'"

Donald opened his eyes and became absolutely still.

"It's your wife," Sandy said.

"Myra," Donald asked, "is it really you?"

"Don't be an idiot. Of course it's me," Sandy said, his voice an octave higher than usual. "I'm watching you, you old fool. I see you flirting."

"Me?" Donald squeaked, sounding so shocked even Sandy couldn't repress a smile.

No one needed the spirit world, Rebecca thought, for that insight about Donald Luff. She was beginning to squirm with annoyance at this time-waster. She wondered if she could announce a sudden headache and leave.

"Yes, you," Sandy continued in his high voice. "You can flirt now, but I'll be here waiting for you."

"Waiting? You mean"—Donald swallowed hard—"soon?"

"No, you old coot. You'll have many years of fun."

"Myra, I don't mean—"

"Donald," Sandy said in his own voice. "She's gone now."

With that, Donald took a deep breath.

What a sham, Rebecca thought, disgusted by how gullible these people were. At $500 per session, no less.

"We have a wonderful group here—very open," Sandy said. You're making my job a complete pleasure. Tell me, are you up for trying to reach someone else?"

Rebecca watched the others give a hearty, "Yes," clearly excited about what had just transpired. Despite the dim candlelight, Rebecca saw Sandy's pale gaze turn to her. With an inward sigh, she nodded.

"Okay, then. Deep breaths, everyone," Sandy said, as he again talked them into relaxing.

He then began to call for a spirit to join them. He called again and again until … "I see a form coming closer."

Everyone again went on high alert.

"I can see … it's a man. And … I can feel … he's touching his head … or is it his heart?"

Cute, Rebecca thought. Now Sandy and the spirit are playing charades.

"He's trying hard to speak."

She hoped he didn't mumble like the spirits the other night.

"There's someone here he wants to talk to. That he desperately wants to talk to, but I'm not sure what he's saying. I think it's a 'ja' sound."

Sandy either needs a clearer connection, or he's simply using the same old material over and over.

"He's an older man, but strong. Yes, very strong. And tall. He works with his hands," Sandy continued. "Perhaps with the land. A farm—that's it. He's a farmer."

A farmer?

That caught Rebecca's full attention.

"He's rubbing his chest as if, perhaps, it hurts or once hurt him."

His heart? Her stomach began to tighten.

"His name—the 'ja' sound was part of *his* name!" Sandy cried.

Benjamin?

"Oh, my God!" a woman's voice cried.

What the hell? Rebecca glared at the woman holding Sandy's left hand, a newcomer named Ellen Fiddler. She wanted nothing so much as to tell the woman to shut up and butt out.

"It's my husband, George," Ellen whispered. She was mousy-looking behind white-framed glasses, with short, curly gray hair. "He died of a heart attack eight months ago."

Sandy looked startled. "Your husband was a farmer?"

"A gentleman farmer, he liked to say. He owned the land and paid others to do the work."

"Hello, Ellen." The voice came out of Sandy's mouth, but it was deeper than usual, and slightly slurred. "I've missed you so much."

Ellen stared at him in shock. "That doesn't

sound like George."

"Hush!" Marta said. "It's his spirit, not his body that's here. Do you want to talk to him or not?"

Ellen's eyes widened. She gulped, then nodded.

Rebecca's cheeks burned with self-deprecation. Just like that, she nearly fell for this scam, too. She shuddered as she realized just how close she had come to speaking, to jumping in and joining needy desperados. But that was it: this whole ideology played on a very basic human need. A "ja" sound and a bad heart? We *want* to believe, she thought.

But, if all that were true, how the hell had Sandy come so close to guessing her father's name? To knowing the way he had died?

Sandy was busy asking Ellen questions that led to her revealing that George was still being bothered by his mother-in-law in the afterlife. Ellen softly admitted her mother never cared much for George in this life either.

Then, after more talk and many tears shed by Ellen, Sandy sat back and let go of her hand.

Everyone else let go of each other as well. He then put his hand on the woman's arm. "It'll be all right, Ellen."

She sniffed and nodded her head, at the same time tried to wipe tears from her cheeks. "I'm sorry I hogged your séance. I suppose other people wanted a chance to talk, too."

"It's not my séance, my dear, but yours," Sandy said. "All I can say is, I felt such overwhelming love and joy coming from that spirit, I can't even begin to tell you. I'm sure it was George, and he wanted you to know he's all right, he's even happy where he is, and he looks forward to the day when you're together again."

"Oh." Her eyes widened. "But I remarried two months ago. I know it was soon, but I thought it would be wrong to chance losing him. His name's Tom. He's also a good man."

"Remarried?" Sandy mugged a stricken look for the others at the table. "It sounds as if she's going to have a very busy afterlife."

Everyone laughed at that, and the tension in the room vanished. Lucian used it as his cue to turn on the lights.

"That was wonderful!" Sandy said to everyone. "What a fabulous group! This was a marvelous experience for me as well. And Ellen"— he stood, pulled her to her feet, and kissed her cheek—"it was an absolute joy to bring you a message from the beyond."

Lucian then wheeled in a cart filled with expensive chocolates and small desserts along with wine, tea, and coffee. Everyone was invited to stay, eat, and share with Sandy and each other what they saw and felt during the séance.

Rebecca listened as the married Sandoristas, Marta and Henry, talked to Ellen about her feelings after experiencing her first encounter with the other side. Ellen said she was now quite "flummoxed" about Tom and the fact that she remarried so quickly. Was it a mistake? No one could get a word in as she debated, mostly with herself, about her marriages.

Rebecca shook her head and walked away. What a soap opera.

She saw that everyone was interested in talking about what they had experienced. She had no idea that she was supposed to have been doing her own bit of channeling, but she wasn't surprised to see several of them try to top each other as to how much of a "presence" they felt. Even those who initially said they'd felt nothing, were soon nodding and—*oh my God, what a surprise!*—realized that they, too, had witnessed the spirit's arrival.

Donald Luff walked up to her with a glass of white wine. "For you," he said, handing it to her.

She guessed he had forgotten her hand squeeze or, God forbid, thought she was trying to show she liked him. "Thank you."

"What did you think of the evening?" he asked. "Did you find it wonderful?"

"It was interesting," she admitted. "But many of these people spent a lot of money and had no contact with the other side. I wonder how they feel."

"That's no problem at all." He beamed. "I often make no contact, but I'm always honored to be able to contribute my abilities to help someone else realize what a wonderful world not only this one is, but that there's another even greater and more magnificent waiting for all of us. It fills me with joy. And I'll do all I can to help you feel it, too."

"How lovely," she said, her sarcasm going unnoticed.

She felt a hand on her arm and turned to find Sandy behind her. "I would love to know what you thought of all this," he said softly. "Cocktails?"

"Sure."

She noticed Donald frown at the two of them and then march away to talk to Ellen Fiddler.

Sandy leaned close to Rebecca. "Ignore him. He's the Lothario of the séance circuit."

"There's a circuit?"

"Most definitely. Give me a minute, then we can get out of here."

Sandy announced to the group that they could stay and talk as long as they wished, and that Lucian would lock up. He said he was exhausted from the ordeal of conjuring up two spirits, but if any of them would like to return next Thursday night, to let him know right now, along with a deposit for half the fee, because the session would fill up as soon as it was announced.

Six of the other séance participants descended on him with checks and credit cards. Rebecca looked around for the one other participant besides herself who wasn't signing up. "Where's Candace?" she asked Marta. "Did she leave?"

"She said she suddenly wasn't feeling well." Gloria, a newcomer, jumped in with the answer. "I think she went to the ladies."

"Did I hear Candace isn't feeling well?" Sandy asked. "Could someone check on her to make sure she's all right?"

"I'll go!" Gloria looked ecstatic to do anything for Sandy.

He went back to taking credit cards when a muffled scream was heard. It no sooner registered than Gloria pulled open the door to the conference room. "She's dead!"

oOo

Richie had heard that Rebecca was in court most of the day on a murder case she'd been involved in last year. He knew better than to phone to talk about ghosts and spirits. Or about Sandy Geller and why she seemed to be spending so much time with him.

In any case, he much preferred to see her, face-to-face, after court let out. But that evening, again, she wasn't answering her phone.

He drove out to her apartment to see if she was home, but her SUV wasn't on the street.

He wondered why.

He tried calling several more times that evening—at ten o'clock, eleven, midnight. After the club closed at two a.m., on the way home he swung by Mulford Alley. Rebecca's SUV still wasn't there.

Chapter 11

Rebecca had never realized, when on the "other" side of a homicide investigation, just how slowly everything moved.

The moment Gloria cried out that Candace was dead, everyone seemed to freeze until Sandy stood. "What do you mean, dead?"

"I'll take a look," Rebecca told him. "It's your job to make sure everyone stays put."

Sandy's mouth dropped open, but then he nodded. "Will do."

"Stays put?" Donald asked, moving towards Rebecca. "What do you mean?"

She didn't answer, but went into the bathroom. There were three stalls. Candace was on the floor, the door to her stall still fastened shut.

Rebecca used her small lock set to open it. The woman looked like she had suffered convulsions and vomiting, but there were no signs of a physical attack.

Rebecca called Homicide and the Crime Scene

Unit. As she returned to the main room, she showed her badge as she explained what was happening.

Before long, her phone buzzed. Homicide Inspector Paavo Smith and his partner, Toshiro "Yosh" Yoshiwara, were on call that night. "Rebecca," Paavo said. "Dispatch told me you're at the crime scene. What's going on?"

"I'm not sure. It could be natural causes—a violent heart attack, perhaps, but I just don't know."

"We've got an active murder scene going," he said. "It'll be an hour before we can get away. Are you in a position to handle the case?"

"'Fraid not. It's a ... a get-together, and I was invited here. So, I could be considered as much of a suspect as anyone else in the room."

"Got it. A couple uniforms are on their way to secure the crime scene. Any danger in waiting for us to get there?"

She looked over the mostly geriatric group. "I don't think so."

Just then, Lucian led the uniformed police into the room and Rebecca ended the call to talk to them.

She began writing down everyone's name, address, and phone number, as well as checking their I.D.s. Even though she was theoretically a suspect, she knew it had to be done, and she was saving time taking care of it herself.

Evelyn Ramirez, the medical examiner, had been at the murder scene with Paavo and Yosh, so she didn't arrive at Sandy's offices until shortly before the homicide inspectors did. All were already pretty worn out from working the earlier crime scene. They gave no details, but it sounded ugly and bloody.

Paavo and Yosh talked to Sandy and others in the meeting room while Ramirez checked over the body. When the two inspectors and Rebecca went to see how Ramirez was doing, she wearily rose to her feet.

"Everything is consistent with a heart attack," the M.E. said as she peeled off her latex gloves. "I'll look her over again back at the morgue, but short of doing a full autopsy, I'd say that's what we've got. Given her age, and all, unless your investigations point to something more, I think 'natural causes' is a very safe conclusion."

Paavo faced Rebecca, waiting for her reaction. She wasn't sure what to say to him. Paavo was, she readily admitted, her favorite fellow inspector. Smart, tough, and very good-looking, he was a cop's cop. Plus, when she was new in homicide, he showed her how to be good at her job in the real world—something much more valuable than months of classroom or theoretical training could ever be. That she, romantically speaking, never had a chance with him from the time he first met Richie Amalfi's cousin, Angie, was one of the bane's of Rebecca's love life.

She drew in her breath. "I haven't heard anything that would make me think there's foul play going on," she admitted. But even as she said it, something niggled at her.

"But?" Yosh asked. He was Japanese-American, large, burly, and as boisterous and jolly as Paavo was quiet and serious. "Come on, Rebecca. We can all tell something's got your dander up. What's going on?"

"Nothing."

"Might it have to do with séances?" Yosh

didn't bother to hide his grin. "What's going on here, Mayfield? You going to start looking into crystal balls to solve your cases?"

She grimaced. "Funny. I was invited here, that's all."

"Ah. I see," Yosh said. "Actually, I don't. What are you up to?"

"Nothing! It's late. You guys are tired, and so am I. I think the CSI should check a couple of things, though."

"Check for what?" Yosh asked. "Is this a crime scene or not? I say we continue to talk to the people out there, and if nothing seems off, we wrap it up. If something more is apparent, we get CSI involved. Until then, they've got a lot going on tonight."

She faced Paavo.

"Yosh is right, Rebecca," Paavo said. "We'll cordon this off as a crime scene until we're sure what we've got going. But you do look like something's troubling you."

"It's a good plan," she admitted. "I'll leave the questioning to you guys."

"And we'll question you as well," Yosh said.

"I can't wait to find out, officially, why you're at a séance." With that, he let out one of his big belly laughs.

Rebecca couldn't help but cringe.

oOo

The next morning, even though it was Saturday and Rebecca was off duty, she went to Homicide.

It was about 3 a.m. before she got home last night, but even then, she couldn't sleep.

Her mind kept going over similarities between Candace's death and that of Neda Fourman and the women Richie told her about. And she kept remembering how pleasant and full of life Candace had been.

Of course, sudden, natural deaths happened all the time. But still…

Rebecca knew she couldn't enjoy her weekend with this death preying on her mind. That was the reason for showing up at work that morning.

She no sooner sat down at her desk than her boss, Lt. Eastwood, arrived. He was never there on Saturdays. He stopped in front of her. "I thought you'd be here," he said. "I came in to hear, first hand, why you were at last night's murder scene. A séance? Really? Let's go into my office."

She sat across from his desk feeling like a naughty child facing the principal. She explained that she was at the séance only because a friend had asked her to attend.

"That's a relief," Eastwood said. "I somehow can't see you as a séance goer. I'm not sure that would be such a good activity for a homicide inspector in any case."

"Yes, sir," she said. She knew he'd been skeptical of her ever since her little run-in with the Russian mob. Not to mention her apparently never-ending association with Richie.

She went on to explain that by the time Paavo, Yosh, and the M.E. had finished questioning Sandy and the séance participants the night before, they had pretty much concluded that Candace Carter had died of natural causes. But Rebecca was aware of other similar deaths surrounding followers of Sandor Geller. As such, she wanted to pursue the case a bit further. She didn't want to be thought of as stepping on anyone's toes, however.

"How were you made aware of those other

deaths?" he asked.

She wasn't sure how to answer. "From a confidential informant, sir. That information was, in fact, the reason I was at the séance."

He frowned at her, but didn't demand she give up her source. "Are you sure you trust this 'informant' enough to get involved?"

"What if he's right? I've had good tips before."

Eastwood thought a moment, and then told her that if she truly believed something there was worth investigating, he wouldn't forbid it. But it was off the books, on her own, and he would authorize no overtime unless some clear sign of foul play turned up. He also didn't want Sutter to help.

She wondered if he honestly thought that last point would matter in the least. Sutter's on-the-job retirement made him a hindrance more than anything.

Back at her desk, she called up everything she could find about both Candace and Neda, including looking into Kenneth Neary, whose "ghost" had come to Neda Fourman when she took part in Geller's séances. From all she could learn about the man, he'd been married twice, and his last marriage was a strong one. There was no indication of him ever having anything to do with Neda.

Rebecca debated talking to his widow, but couldn't imagine that leading anywhere useful for either of them.

She then looked into Candace Carter.

She called the mortuary and asked if anyone had inquired about Candace and was given the name of a woman who had referred to herself as a friend. Rebecca phoned the woman, Mary Rodriguez, and said she would like to visit her shortly with a few questions about Candace.

Rebecca was just about to leave Homicide when who should walk in but Richie.

Rebecca found she was actually glad to see him. He'd been on her mind a lot since Thursday's strange FBI visit. Now that she'd been told something about his 'work,' she had questions. Lots of questions.

"How are you doing, Inspector?" he asked.

She was surprised at his formality. "Fine. I was hoping to talk to you."

"About Sandy Geller, I guess," he said as he sat down in the guest chair beside her desk.

"You've been spending a lot of time with him, I hear."

Her brows lifted. "Wherever did you hear that?"

"Word gets around."

She pursed her lips. "I've been spending time to find out what he's been up to."

"Until late at night?"

What's going on with him? She cocked her head. "Are you having me watched?"

He raised his hands, palms up. "I'm innocent. I know nothing but what I hear."

Tempting as it was to needle him, she said, "If you heard about last night, you'd know one of his clients died after attending a séance."

His eyes widened at the news. "You're shitting me. Was it an old lady?"

"She was getting up there, but seemed remarkably healthy … until she wasn't. Her body is in the morgue in case we want an autopsy done. I just need a reason."

"Christ! It doesn't seem to be healthy to have anything to do with Geller. Hope you're being careful around him."

"Of course, but he doesn't seem—"

"He's an actor. He makes his living being not what he seems."

She hated to admit it, but he had a point. "You may be right. Anyway, I'm going to visit a couple of the deceased woman's friends. See what they can tell me about her."

"Mind if I come along?"

"Yes, I mind. You have no business coming with me on a case."

"Oh. So, this is a case now, is it?"

He had her there. "Maybe not yet."

An eyebrow rose at her admission. "Look, I know more about this situation than anyone. Plus, I've learned some new stuff about Geller from Shay."

"What stuff?"

He simply stared at her with those dark, heavy-lidded eyes.

She grimaced because she knew that unless he came along, he wouldn't be telling her much about what he and Shay were finding out. In fact, he might decide to check out Sandy on his own, which could cause all kinds of complications. She could be doing herself, Homicide, maybe even the entire city, a favor by keeping him near her. Or so she hoped.

"Okay, Richie. You can join me as long as you promise not to say a word. You're there to observe *only*."

"Whatever you want, Inspector," he said. "Your wish is my command."

She didn't believe that for a minute.

o0o

Mary Rodriguez lived in the flat above Candace's. When the landlord was informed of Candace's death, he had immediately told Mary since the two women had been close at one time. Mary had also invited their mutual friend, Jean Hu, to come to her home to be with her when the police arrived and to possibly offer insights of her own.

Rebecca introduced herself, showing her badge. She then introduced Richie as her associate and noticed that the two women didn't bat an eye, but simply accepted his presence.

Mary invited them into the cozy living room, and they sat.

"Have you known Candace very long?"

Rebecca asked.

"Oh, yes," Mary said. Jean nodded in agreement. "For years, we weren't only neighbors, but we went to the same Unitarian Church as Candace and her sister, Pearl."

"I see," Rebecca said.

"Candace stopped attending after Pearl died. We've seen less and less of her ever since."

"When was that?" Rebecca asked, taking notes.

"It was a couple of years back."

"Was Pearl's death sudden?" Richie asked. Rebecca gave him "the look" to remind him he said he wouldn't interfere, but he shrugged it off.

"She'd been sickly for years—overweight, diabetic, heart issues. Her death was no surprise, believe me."

"What can you tell me about Candace's involvement with Sandy Geller?"

Jean's eyebrows rose as she looked at Mary. Mary drew in her breath and then spoke. "A few years back, the four of us took in one of Geller's shows. While Pearl and the two of us found the show amusing, something about it 'spoke' to

Candace, and she went back a couple more times. After Pearl died, all that changed."

"How do you mean?" Rebecca asked.

"You need to understand, I guess, that Candace and Pearl had been constant companions, even taking vacations together—sometimes their husbands went along, and sometimes the men stayed home. The "girls" as they called themselves didn't care, as long as they were together. They talked all the time on the phone, lived a block from each other, and seemed to share every waking thought. And neither had children.

"Anyway, after Pearl's death, we saw Candace less and less, and she only went to lunch with us when we refused to take no for an answer. She was spending most of her time attending séances and getting to know people who believed in them. We were worried about her, but when we tried to talk about it, she said we were being silly. She insisted Sandy's séances were nothing like the nonsense shown in Hollywood movies, but his were real, and spirits really did come and talk to them. Including her sister."

"She actually said her dead sister talked to

her?" Richie asked.

"Yes. Her words scared us, but Candace said she felt sorry for us, that our minds were closed off to what the world was really all about. She said that, for the first time since Pearl's death, she was happy."

"She was widowed, right?" Rebecca asked.

"Yes, for many years. Candace once confessed that she hadn't bothered to connect with her husband's spirit. She had tolerated the man for thirty-two years and felt nothing but relief when he died."

Richie caught Rebecca's eye at that, and gave her a "what is it with you women?" look.

Rebecca shook her head, attempted to look annoyed, but failed miserably. At least she didn't smile.

Jean Hu finally spoke up. "I tried to question Candace," Jean said, "to show her that what she was hearing at these séances was all fake. But she used facts to prove it was all real."

"Facts?" Rebecca asked.

"Candace claimed she and Pearl talked about things that only they could possibly know about.

They talked of their trips to watch the leaves turn in New England, and a ride on a Mississippi River steamboat. After that, Candace became a complete believer in Sandor Geller and his séances."

"Did either of you," Richie asked, "ever attend a séance with Candace?"

Both women shook their heads, looking horrified at the thought.

o0o

"We need to talk to someone who attended one of those séances," Richie said as they left the Rodriguez home and headed back to Richie's car. Rebecca sometimes felt she ought to drive her SUV for police business, but considering he owned a Porsche, who could blame her? "Someone who might know if Geller used leading questions that made Candace think she was talking to her sister."

"If?" Rebecca asked as she got into the Porsche. She knew she was setting herself up for a heckling, but said, "I attended one of his séances, the one in which Candace Carter died. That's all Geller does is lead. People want to believe what they want to believe, and if he can help them do it, they're grateful. That's all that's going on there."

Richie went completely still. He had been about to put on his seatbelt, but instead his hand froze in mid-air still holding the clasp. "You did *what?*"

Her lips tightened. "You heard me. So?"

"Nothing." He snapped the seatbelt in place. "So why didn't you just ask Neda Fourman how she died?" Then he laughed.

"I knew you'd say that." She fumed. "I just knew it. Okay, then, you said you want to talk to séance-goers, I'll give you séance-goers."

They first went to Marta and Henry Highfield's home in the expensive Marina district. The couple was surprised to learn that Rebecca was continuing to investigate what they had understood was a death by natural causes. Nevertheless, they were more than willing to help.

Henry seemed a bit skeptical about Richie being there, but Marta had nothing but smiles for him and seemed rather taken by his good looks and expensive clothes. She said she was gratified to hear the police and their 'consultants' were waking up to psychic phenomena.

They sat in the living room. Marta served

coffee. Both Highfields expressed happiness that Candace and Pearl were together again, after how desperately lonely Candace had been. Perhaps, Henry mused, Pearl had been quietly attending last night's séance, and had opened the door to bring Candace home to her.

"I take it you're a Sandorista," Richie said to Marta. He sat on the loveseat adjacent to the end of the sofa on which Marta sat.

"Yes. Isn't that a cute name?" she replied, reaching out and placing her diamond ring laden hand on his arm. "Yes, Henry and I are happy to follow Sandy. He's a wonderful man."

"Was Candace a Sandorista as well?" he asked.

"She thought so," Marta told him. "She did enjoy the meetings, but they did stretch her budget, from what I understand." She pulled back her hand but continued to eye Richie as if he was tutti-frutti and she just loved ice cream.

"She often said she had to scrimp to attend a séance," Henry added, "but she managed to get to all the ones Sandy invited her to. In fact, I heard that Sandy gave her a big break on the cost of admission."

"He's such a darling man!" Marta gushed.

He's a peach all right, Rebecca thought, convinced that Richie's supposedly outlandish suspicions had a basis in fact. Now, all she needed was proof of something illegal, like murder, going on.

Marta faced Richie. "Can I invite you to one of our séances, Mr. Amalfi? I'm sure you'll be amazed by all you'll witness and learn."

"No doubt about that." He turned towards Rebecca. "I think it's time we get going. Don't we have more stops to make?"

She thanked the Highfields for their assistance and left. Even as they got into Richie's Porsche, she was still inwardly laughing at his expression over being invited to a séance.

oOo

Richie was glad to learn the next Sandorista on Rebecca's list was also the last. He didn't know how much more of this hocus-pocus stuff he could take.

Donald Luff lived in an expensive apartment at the foot of Van Ness Avenue. Richie hoped he was more normal than the other Sandoristas had been.

He didn't care for the way Luff grabbed Rebecca's hands and kissed her cheek as if they were long-lost friends when they'd known each other less than 24-hours. Nor did he like the way Luff frowned at him and then proceeded to ignore completely ignore him as he led them into his living room. The apartment had a great view of Alcatraz Island and the Golden Gate.

"I know you're here about Candace, but I'm sorry to say, *Rebecca,*" Luff said, emphasizing his familiar use of her first name, as he snuck a peek in Richie's direction, "that I paid no attention at all to the woman. She was too old for me." At that, he chortled.

As if, Richie thought.

"Can you think of anything at all—or if anyone seemed particularly interested in her, or disliked her?" Rebecca asked. "Did you notice anything that might have seemed a bit off?"

"The only thing off to me was that she was always talking about missing her sister. Her sister was a nice lady, I'm sure, but shouldn't Candace have been missing a man?" His eyebrows waggled at Rebecca, making Richie want to smash his face in. "That's more normal."

"You never know." Rebecca looked disgusted and quickly turned to Richie. "I think it's time—"

"No kidding!" Richie jumped to his feet.

"You know, Rebecca," Luff said, taking her arm as he walked her to the door. The little twerp barely reached her nose. "I often think better later in the day. In the evening, in fact. Maybe after a cocktail or two. And some dancing. You know, there's a great new nightclub in town. Lots of people talk about it. They play some old favorites from my day. New stuff, too, but I like a Gershwin tune. How about you? How about tonight, in fact?" He let her go to do a little cha-cha-cha step. "Let's face the music and dance, Rebecca! I can't remember the name of the place, but I'll find it. Once there, my memories of Candace Carter might take a turn for the better."

"It's called Big Caesar's," Richie said as he opened the door and whisked Rebecca into the hallway. "And she's already been there."

Chapter 12

I may need to change my club's image if aging Casanovas like Donald Luff think it's the place to go." Richie held the car door open for Rebecca.

"Big Caesar's image is just fine," Rebecca said as she got into the passenger seat. "Better than fine."

He could see the turmoil she felt over him using old-fashioned manners with her, as if a part of her thought she should pull her own damn door shut, but another enjoyed the lady-like treatment. She'd once confessed that it was tiring to always have to act like a ball-busting cop, but that it was necessary in her position.

She let him shut the door.

"Where to now?" he said as he got into the driver's seat.

She met his gaze a moment, then looked away. "Somewhere we can talk."

"Sounds serious."

She faced forward. "Hard to know."

He headed to Union Street where the bars and eateries were less touristy and crowded than in the better known parts of the city. He stopped at a bistro where they found a table in a dimly lit corner. He ordered a beer, Rebecca a glass of chardonnay. Neither was hungry.

"So," Richie said when the drinks were delivered. "What's up?"

She took a sip of her wine, then kept her fingers on the stem of the glass. "You mentioned that you and Shay learned something about Geller's finances."

Something told him that wasn't the cause of her discomfort. He told her about Shay's discovery that Geller had millions sitting in Swiss bank accounts, but also several million dollars in banks in this country. And, from one such accounts he was sending money each month to eight men and women who had once been customers but nearly bankrupted themselves going to his séances. Geller now allowed them to attend a séance free-of-charge every few months.

"Eight people?" Rebecca was speechless.

"At this very moment," he said, "Shay is trying

to find out more about the people now being paid, and also to track down all those who were paid in the past but are now dead."

"What makes you think there are any?"

He cocked his head. "What makes you think there aren't? We don't know how long he's been doing this."

She nodded. "I don't get it. If he's in this for the money, how does giving away money help him?"

"I don't get it either," Richie admitted. "But if the answer is in his bank accounts, Shay will find out. We just need to be patient."

"True."

He reached for her hand and squeezed it gently. He never thought he'd find a cop's hands to be so soft, or so touchable. "Now tell me why we're really here," he said, letting her go.

Big blue eyes lifted to meet his. She looked troubled. He stiffened, knowing he wasn't going to like what was coming. "I heard something about you. About how you make your money."

"Yeah? Who d'you hear it from?" he asked.

"I'm not saying. What's important is what I

heard—that you're a 'fixer.'" She shifted back from the table. "Is it true?"

He fidgeted with the black leather band on his Piaget watch, sliding it back and forth on his wrist. "I guess I should have explained, but I didn't think you'd understand."

"Try me."

His jaw tightened. Before he said anything, before he told her anything more about his life, he had to ask—even though he suspected he wouldn't like her answer whether it was a "yes" or a "no." He asked, "Does it matter?"

She looked pained. "It shouldn't. You know that as well as I do. And I wish it didn't." She held his gaze. "But I want to hear, from you, that what you're doing doesn't cross the line. I think I've made it clear that I don't care what others speculate or say about you, but if I can't trust you, I'll walk away and not look back."

His shoulders sagged. "How many times do I have to tell you the same thing?"

She looked stunned, but then nodded. "You're right. It's not fair. But if I didn't care, I wouldn't ask."

"That's honest," he admitted, knowing what it cost her to admit feeling anything about him.

She leaned closer. "You're like a bad penny—you keep coming back. And I keep letting you. Do you know how stupid you make me feel?"

"Yeah, I do." He took her hands, both of them this time. "Because I'm the one who keeps coming up with reasons to see you."

She shook her head and gave a half-smile. "What am I going to do with you?"

"Want a suggestion?" He grinned, and he found himself smugly pleased that, by her expression, she seemed to like the path his mind had traveled down.

But then she pulled her hands free. "What I want is simply to know what you're all about."

He had the waitress bring them refills, and after she did so, he began to explain.

"You know I grew up poor," he said. Rebecca nodded. "No time or money for more than a couple classes at San Francisco Junior College, which I hated. So I knocked around from one lousy job to another, including working for a bail bondsman, Abe Pollard of Pollard and Seider."

"I know them," Rebecca said. "They've been around forever."

"Yeah, well, I did any shit thing Abe wanted—like watching some of his less trustworthy bails twenty-four seven to make sure they didn't skip, seeing who they were hanging around with, taking photos of the collateral as well as the people who put it up. The whole nine yards.

"The good part was—and I didn't even realize it for a few years—I met a lot of people doing that, important people. On one side were the supposed good guys: DAs, ADAs, judges, lawyers of all types, and a lot of cops. And then there was the other side, mainly, Abe's clients. Most were scum—not worth the time of day, and guilty as sin. But other times, as Abe became one of the few people in the city who could afford to take a risk with a bail of a few hundred-thousand dollars, and eventually, bails that hit a million or more, the clients became more interesting than anything else going on. Do you follow?"

She nodded. "I'm usually on the other side, working with the DA to get the bail as high as possible, but I've seen the risk the bondsmen have to take on some of these cases, and what goes into them deciding if it's worth the risk or not. So did you become a bail bondsman yourself?"

"Hell no! No way I wanted the stress of that job. Especially with those big bail cases, they can go on for years before they go to trial. All that time, the bondsman's money is at risk. Even with insurance, the collateral itself causes risks. Real estate can tank, the price of gold can nose dive, whatever. On top of that, if the client flies the coop, or even goes 'missing' for too long, it can cost. I'm not putting my money on a guy who's already, in many cases, proven to be a thief, a killer, or a nice guy who's gotten in over his head—and sometimes those 'nice' ones are the biggest flight risk because they're so scared of what's going to happen to them."

"Makes sense," she said.

He studied her, trying to gauge her reaction. If she looked like she didn't understand, or worse, looked down her nose at his story, he would stop, pay for the drinks, and take her the hell back to work. But so far, those blue eyes weren't judgmental. He continued. "One thing I learned from Abe, was a sense of who to trust—who he'd think would stick around, and who might run. Of course, things happened in life and someone he'd swear would show up for court was suddenly half way around the world. But a lot of the job was about reading people, and Abe was good at that."

Richie took a quick swallow of some beer. "So anyway, I was making all kinds of connections doing this. And one day, one of them goes to Abe and says he's got a big problem but doesn't want anyone to know. He's wondering if Abe could make a deal with the law outside the books. Abe was up to his eyeballs in cases and asked me if I wanted to help the guy out. The guy was a big name in sports around here. With the 49ers, in fact. He'd gotten into a bar fight, broke another guy's nose. The one with the broken nose threatened to press charges and sue. It could have gotten really ugly for the football player. I met with the 49er. All that was needed was for someone to talk to the other guy, calm him down, make him an offer to get him to go away. There was no need to involve the law at all. Two guys fighting. Big deal. It would have been nothing if one of the two didn't have very deep pockets.

"I talked to the nose guy. He'd decided his broken nose was worth five million dollars. I convinced him it was worth two hundred thousand—which was about ten times what it was really worth. But the football player wanted it to all go away. It did. I took a cut; and that was that. I could not believe how much money I made just for talking."

She grinned at that, and nodded as if to say, "Go on." He did.

"It turns out ball players are forever getting themselves in jams, trust me on that. And they do not want cops involved." With that, he sat back in his chair, his dark eyes never leaving hers.

She looked down at her wine. "And that's what you do," she said, slowly rotating the glass. "Help ball players make problems go away."

"Baseball, football, basketball, college, pros—we've got a lot of teams in the area. Plus sportscasters, people on TV or movies, politicians, all people who can't afford bad PR. Then there are those in charge of corporations, hospitals, non-profits—you name it. A lot of the high tech millionaires around here are kids, and they get into all kinds of garbage, usually involving sex or drugs. Mistresses who get bossy and want a wedding ring or money—basically, blackmailers—cause tremendous problems. So that's what I do. I spend my time being helpful, making things better for people." He shrugged. "I'm a nice guy. What can I say?"

She looked worried. "Yes, I'm sure you are, until the other party doesn't want the problem fixed. Many of them, I suspect, want the publicity, or vengeance, and are happy to ruin your client's life or career. That's where it's easy to go over the line. I've seen it, Richie, and I know you have as well."

He scrapped at the beer bottle label with his thumbnail. But it was stubborn, and he pushed it aside. "I don't do that. Never have. I know it's a slippery slope, and I've seen people slide down it very, very quickly. Sure, I have to do some leaning on people, threaten counter suits, dig up dirt and swear I'll use it. But if the other person won't back down, I tell my client the truth. Leaning too hard would only make it worse. In those cases, I don't charge a penny, no matter how much time I've spent, how much investigating I've done. I walk away as if I've never been involved."

"But things can still go south quickly," she said.

"Things can go south when you're running a candy store. That's why I don't work with anyone unless I feel that my client, at least, can be trusted."

"Always?"

"Yes."

"You've got cases going on now?" she asked.

"I've always got cases going on." His voice was flat.

She sat, staring at the table top a moment, then finished her wine. "Okay. We should get going. I've got things to do in Homicide."

He left money on the table as they stood, put their jackets on, and left the bistro.

They said nothing until they reached his car. He couldn't take the silence. He turned her to face him and kept his hands on her arms. "I told you what you wanted to know. So, where do I stand?"

"I'm not sure," she said. "It's a lot to take in."

"You knew I wasn't out there selling Amway

products."

She smiled at that, and he imagined she must be thinking of him going to door-to-door with a suitcase stuffed with cleaning aids. But then she lifted eyes that made his heart do funny things and surprised him by asking, "What I don't get is, why do you care what I think?"

Good question. He stepped even closer. He was expecting her to push him away, at a minimum. More likely, deck him with a karate chop. But instead she swayed towards him, and that was more than he could resist. He kissed her. And she let him.

Big mistake. The scent of her, the feel of her body against his … he remembered what it was like months ago at his house, how he hadn't wanted to let her go then, and didn't want to now. But they were standing on a sidewalk near Union Street. He let her go and held the car door open for her to get in.

He darted around his car and jumped into the driver's seat, ready to drive as fast as traffic laws and his Porsche would allow back to his house, not even bothering with his seat belt.

"Take me to Homicide," she said.

His hand paused over the Start button. *"Now?"*

"I've got work to do. The more I think about it, an autopsy should be done on Candace Carter. I've got to talk to the M.E."

She didn't look at him, but stared straight ahead.

For some reason, he understood. He did as she asked.

Chapter 13

Rebecca had no sooner sat down at her desk than Agent Brandon Seymour showed up.

"It's Saturday," she said. "I thought the federal government shut down on weekends."

"Not me. Let's talk in private."

She rolled her eyes and led him to the conference room they had used last time.

"What did you find out?" he asked before she even sat.

She folded her arms. "I take it you're asking about Amalfi?"

"I saw him come here earlier, and then the two of you left together."

"Yes, well, I didn't learn anything you don't already know," she said.

"Did you ask about Claire Baxter?"

"Of course not." She gave a slight shake of the head, wondering how she'd gotten into this mess with Seymour. "He'd wonder how in the world I knew her name, let alone anything else. And I don't appreciate being spied on. And I know Richie would hate it."

"No one is spying on you. We're worried about Amalfi. National security can be involved."

"Bull shit."

He smiled. He actually looked almost human when he smiled. "You're right. But saying that often works with people. Still, if you hear anything at all about Claire Baxter, Middle Eastern artwork, art smuggling, and so on, be sure to let me know."

"I still think you're wasting your time," she said.

"But Claire Baxter is with him a lot. Maybe it's personal between them."

She didn't like the way he was staring at her, and couldn't help but wonder if Richie's surprising kiss—very sweet, very chaste, but filled with a pulse-quickening promise—hadn't now found its way into some national database. She did her best not to show any expression as she said, "Maybe so."

Agent Seymour left to return to snooping on people, and she went back to work.

Seymour's visit irritated her on a number of

levels, and she was too keyed up to do desk work. She decided to go to Sandy Geller's office and see what he had to say about Candace Carter's death. She was also curious about the other women— Neda Fourman and Betty Faroni—but she knew that asking Geller any more questions about Neda, and particularly if she also mentioned Betty, would definitely put him on high alert. Besides, she had a good deal of confidence in Shay's ability to find out what was going on—much more than any other computer technician, aka hacker, she knew of.

She was escorted to Geller's office. He seemed happy to see her until she told him she was looking a bit further into Candace Carter's death. Then, it was as if a light had switched off. All his laughter, smiles, and charm vanished and he turned cold and hard answering only with a crisp "yes" or "no" response, and offering no help whatsoever. He soon glanced at his watch and announced he needed to get ready for that evening's performance at the Geary Street theater and showed her to the door.

She left his office, but rather than leaving the premises altogether, she decided to question Lucian Tully.

She met Sandor's assistant in one of the smaller meeting rooms. It was the first time she'd talked one-on-one with him. His skin was so pale, it was actually distracting.

"How long have you worked for Sandy?" she asked.

He folded long fingers together and gave her a wide-eyed stare. "I've been here five years." His breathing came fast and heavy. "I was one of Sandy's first hires."

"I see that you're twenty-six," she continued. "Are you married or anything?"

"No." He blushed. "I'm way too busy for anyone but Sandy. I'm always there when he needs me." His smile was both proud and shy. As she studied the way he answered, she saw no hint of anything sexual between the two men. If anything, Lucian evinced a juvenile case of hero-worship.

"Did you know Candace Carter very well?"

He blinked a couple of times. "Not really."

"But hasn't she been a client for several years?" Rebecca pressed.

"I suppose. But I leave the clients to Sandy. I'm not good with people. All I remember about

Candace is Pearl is with us now."

"What?" Rebecca was confused.

"That's what she always said. 'Pearl is with us now.'"

Rebecca looked at him a long moment. "Okay. Thanks. That's all for the moment."

Rebecca also questioned Sandy's other staff, but none admitted to knowing anything about Candace other than her face, name, and telephone number.

Rebecca headed home. When she arrived, she considered going to Big Caesar's later that night to see Richie—to help gather information for the FBI, of course. But then she decided that was playing with fire.

Chapter 14

Richie, you're here so early. What's wrong?" Carmela said the next morning as she opened the door to her flat. She was still wearing a bathrobe and hadn't yet put on her make-up. She patted her hair. Even first thing in the morning, it still resembled a stiff helmet, except that one side of it—the side she must have slept on—was squashed down. Combing it probably consisted of doing whatever it took to make it round again.

"I have to talk to you." He walked straight into the kitchen and sat at the table.

"You want coffee, Richie?" she asked, pouring him a cup before he even answered. "What's happening? A new girlfriend maybe?" She put the cup in front of him. "You aren't here so early to give me some good news are you?"

"Of course not, Ma. Sit down."

"Sit? How can I sit? Did you eat breakfast? I've got bacon and eggs. Or maybe French toast? What would you like?"

He was going to refuse, but then realized she'd be in a much better mood after cooking, especially if she also ate. And if he said no, she'd try to figure out why he didn't like her cooking anymore, or if she needed to come up with a more appealing food for him and if so what, instead of listening to what he had to say.

"Bacon and eggs sounds good."

"*Bene!* And I'll even give you three eggs. You used to be fat, back when you let yourself go after the terrible tragedy. But now, you're getting thin. What's going on with you?"

"I wasn't fat." *Well, maybe.* "And now I'm actually going to the gym at least once a week. Sometimes more. I'm not thin; it's that the flab has turned to muscle. I've never felt better." Sometimes he wondered why he even tried to have a normal conversation with her.

"Yeah, well, you might be healthy, but you could use a little more meat on your bones." She added two more slices of bacon to what already seemed to be half a pound.

As she cooked, she told him about going shopping to try to find a present for a baby shower for the daughter-in-law of one of her friends, and how she was getting tired buying all these presents for *other* people's grandkids. He tuned her out as best he could. Soon she put a platter of food in front of him, with toast that she had buttered, and made a smaller plate for herself. "I'll just take a little," she said, sitting across from him as he began to eat, "to keep body and soul together. I'm meeting the girls at noon mass today, and then we're going to lunch after. Why don't you come to church with me, Richie? It'll help."

"One of these days," he said, doing his best not to get distracted from the reason for his visit. "The girls" were her lady friends, all age 60-plus. He pointed at the food with his fork. "This is great, Ma. You make the best eggs."

"Bacon grease. A little dab. When you get married, be sure to tell your wife."

He rolled his eyes. "Sure. But I'm not getting married."

"Your cop girlfriend might have different ideas. Zi' Maria saw you and her out on Union Street yesterday. She said you two looked real friendly."

"Christ, Ma, you got the Italian hotline checking up on me?"

She shrugged. "I have friends."

"First, she's not my girlfriend. And trust me, she wants to get married even less than I do. And never to me."

"Well, I'm glad of that since *she got you shot a couple months ago!* But any woman who doesn't want to marry you has to be *cacootz.*"

It was a Calabrese word for squash, but also was slang for idiot, or "squash head."

"Not really," he said. "Besides, she's got a boyfriend, so forget about her. Anyway, speaking of girlfriends—"

"Yes?" She actually sounded a bit hopeful.

"*Your* girlfriend—I heard some disturbing news about Geri."

He told her he'd heard that Geri was spending a lot of money on Sandor Geller's shows and séances. The one thing he didn't say was where or how he got the information. Being the kind of guy he was, nobody questioned how he found out what he knew. It was just accepted that he did, and every so often, like now with Geri's money, such beliefs

176 | Joanne Pence

were confirmed.

When he finished, a long moment passed in complete silence. "So, I tell you a little about Geri wondering about her sister's money and next thing I know you're looking into how Geri spends her money?" Carmela glared. "Geri can take care of herself."

"Like her sister did?"

"That was different."

"It's more than that," he said. "And isn't there something *you* want to tell me?" he asked.

Her eyes widened innocently—another tell that she was lying. "Me? *Niente.*"

He folded his arms. "No? How about explaining why you're doing the same thing?"

She put down her fork and cast steely black eyes at him. "What are you saying?"

"I know you've gone to that charlatan's séances. I know you've spent money on him. Lots of money."

"How …" she began, but then she pursed her lips and didn't bother to continue. "So, wise guy, you think you know so much, eh?"

He put down his fork as well. "I know plenty! I

know you gotta stop this. What's the matter with you? I know you say all this supernatural garbage interests you, but this is going too far. What are you trying to do? Talk to Pa? After all these years, is that it? You still miss him that much?"

Carmela stood. *"Madonna mia!"* She crossed herself and slapped her palms together, fingers pointed upward as she looked heavenward. "How did I give birth to such a *buttagatz?*"

"I'm not an idiot," he said indignantly. "I have proof."

Fist on hip, she stared hard at him. "Proof. I spit on your proof! That man, that psychic, is nothing. *Stunad!* How stupid do you think I am? Your poor father—let him rest in peace."

"Okay, Ma, calm down and tell me what's going on."

She looked indignant a while longer, then rolled her eyes and sat down again. "I went to two séances, but I did it for Geri. I wanted to see what they were like and see that Sandor Geller up close." Her eyes narrowed and her forefinger tapped the table as she continued. "I knew there was something wrong with him the minute I laid eyes on him. When he smiles at you, you can't see his teeth, and when he laughs, it's too loud and too long."

Richie didn't want to get into that. "And what did you find out about him?"

"He's un gazzo di chooch."

He nearly choked on his coffee. She'd just called Geller a donkey's dick. He agreed.

"We know that after he found out Geri's sister had no more money to go see him," Carmela said, "the big shot gave her a little money each month to help with expenses. Plus, every so often, he let her attend a séance for free. To keep her happy, I guess. But it makes no sense."

"I agree," Richie admitted.

"Geri wanted to find out what the catch was, so she found out how to get invited to his private séances. For a long time, she didn't tell me she was going. But I knew something was up. She's so stubborn, that Geri, she kept saying, 'No, there's nothing.' But I knew better. I could see the lie on her face. Finally, she confessed."

"Confessed?"

"She temporarily moved most of her money to

her sons—under threat of eternal damnation if they touched any of it. Then she went to Sandy in tears and said she could hardly afford to see him anymore, but she wanted to keep going. He knew she was Betty Faroni's sister, of course, and had even connected her with Betty during a couple of séances. Geri laid it on thick and said she'd rather die than no longer be able to visit with spirits."

"Uh oh," was all Richie could say as he heard this. Thoughts of assisted suicide swirled around his head. Was that what was happening?

"Sandy told her he was sorry, but not to do anything rash. That these things had a way of working themselves out. Two days later she found out how."

"Yes?"

"It's a sin against nature, but I don't think it's illegal. I've got a copy." She rummaged through a stack of papers on the corner of the counter, then pulled one out and handed it to him.

As Richie read it, his jaw dropped open.

Chapter 15

Rebecca spent most of Sunday at work learning what she could about Neda Fourman, Candace Carter, and Elisabetta Faroni, and found that when people lived quiet, normal lives, there really wasn't much for the police to be able to find out about them. Even if they did take up with con-artists in their last days.

Agent Seymour, or Bran, as he asked her to call him, phoned her, and she explained again that she had no information for him. God, but he was a pest. Next, she wasted a lot of time explaining to Dr. Evelyn Ramirez why she wanted an autopsy done on a woman that the two homicide inspectors charged with investigating the death had declared her to have died of natural causes. Ramirez explained the cost of an autopsy, and if it wasn't officially authorized, her staff would need to absorb it, which she didn't want to do, yada, yada.

Finally, Ramirez agreed to continue to hold Candace Carter's body in the morgue until Rebecca secured an official request for an autopsy along with the funds to do it.

All in all, Rebecca was quite glad to head for home by late afternoon.

She turned onto her alley and slammed on the brakes. Parked up ahead were a Porsche and a Maserati. Richie and Shay. They were either in their cars, in her back yard, or in her apartment. She should throw them out. And would, except that she wanted to see them. Or, to be honest, she wanted to see Richie.

They weren't in their cars, the breezeway, or the yard. Given the people they sometimes dealt with, and the FBI's concern, she put her hand on her weapon as she unlocked her apartment door, then carefully opened it.

"Don't shoot, Rebecca. It's just us."

She scowled as she entered.

Richie and his creepy friend Shay sat at the small dinette. They were an incongruous pair, particularly in her little apartment—the blond and serious Shay with his wheat-colored jacket and emerald green ascot, looking like he was about to take a constitutional across the moors, and Richie with his cocky grin, casually tousled black hair, and wearing a black wool pullover and gray slacks that were suitable for a wine-and-cheese nosh.

They had Shay's laptop open and angled so that they could both read from it, and in front of each was a bottle of Blue Moon ale.

Spike sat on Richie's lap. He lifted his head, and the little weasel seemed to think about it a moment before he jumped down and ran over to greet her.

She pointedly exchanged greetings with only Shay as she petted her dog, then faced Richie.

"It's bad enough you barge in without being invited, Amalfi, but trying to steal my dog's affections is going too far."

"Can I help it if Spike has good taste?"

She forced her eyes from his. A while back, circumstances caused her to give him keys to her apartment. When she asked him to return them, he pointed out that sometimes a person wanted help, but not necessarily 9-1-1's. She said she had people in her building who'd help her—Kiki Nuñez and Bradley Frisk. He made no comment, but his look said it all, as in, "If you need serious help, do you really think they'd be able to provide it?"

He had a point. She agreed it would be a good idea for him to keep the key for emergencies. This, however, didn't qualify.

After taking off her jacket, and putting her gun away, she took a deep breath before she faced them again. "You have such a beautiful home, Richie," she said, keeping her voice light. And in truth, he did. "Why did you let yourself into mine?"

She could see from his expression that he had a devilish answer to that, but he simply said, "Shay found something important, and I figured it's easier to show you than to try to explain. Besides, I thought you'd be home on a Sunday. You're not on-call today."

How would he even know that? She gave up. "Okay. Let me feed Spike first."

"I fed him," Richie said. "But I'll get you some beer or wine. I brought over a good chardonnay— it's in the fridge. You'll like it, and you might need it once Shay gets started. This is all about numbers."

"Wine sounds good," she said as she took off her boots, and joined the men at the table. Richie had put a chair for her between him and Shay so she could easily see the screen. Her wine was beside the computer and she reached for it, taking a long sip. Something told her that he was right—she was going to need it.

"This," Shay said as he opened a PDF document, "is a life insurance policy that Neda Fourman had from her employer. She worked as a nurse for over forty years and had a really good pension and insurance plan. She made Lucian Tully her beneficiary, and in return, she was given a monthly stipend, plus she could attend a free séance once a month—that alone was worth five-hundred dollars to her."

Rebecca's head was already spinning. "Lucian Tully? Life insurance? What?"

"It means," Richie said, "she sold her life insurance policy in exchange for the money she needs now."

"I thought that sort of thing was illegal," Rebecca said.

"It's actually not," Shay told her. "What you're thinking of are viatical settlements, where the policy holder was close to dying when the transaction was completed. A lot of changes were made to the insurance industry since those were hot investments, back when young men of working age and insured by their employers were dying of AIDS and needed cash. What Geller is doing is closer to what's called a 'life settlement' but instead of a middle man getting involved, Geller is working directly with his customers. He finds ones who have life insurance, but for whatever reason have no family members as beneficiaries. If such a person becomes strapped for cash, Geller offers a way for them to have money now. Sort of like a reverse mortgage, but it doesn't put a person's home at risk. In fact, there's no risk at all to the policy owner. In most of these cases, they like the idea of Geller getting their life insurance policy to 'carry on his good work,' as one of the people wrote right on the policy when he signed it over."

She looked from Richie to Shay and back again. "How in the world did you find out all this?"

"Carmela told me about it," Richie admitted. "Somehow, her friend Geri convinced Sandy that she was all alone in life—no close family, and, now, she had little money. She was visited by

Lucian Tully who said Sandy was concerned about her. Together, they filled out a form. He started asking about other assets she might have. She kept saying she had nothing until he asked about life insurance. She remembered her sister Betty once told her she had one. Something made Geri say she did have a policy. A few days later, Lucian returned with a promise that Sandy would send her five-hundred dollars each month if she signed a form for her life insurance company that, if processed, would make Lucian her beneficiary."

"What?" Rebecca had never heard of such a thing.

"Right. Of course, she didn't sign the form."

Shay chimed in. "Once Richie gave me the information, I knew what to look for. I found that Lucian had been made beneficiary for her sister Betty's life insurance. And I've already tracked down similar beneficiary changes on five of the eight others Geller is sending money to. They're all in their seventies or eighties and relatively healthy. Most have insurance, small policies, from their jobs or pension funds that they probably haven't thought about until Lucian came knocking at their door with an offer of money. Since the monthly stipends they receive come out of Geller's account, Lucian must be Geller's stooge in this, and nothing more."

"The problem," Richie said, "is the monthly stipend. If the client doesn't die quickly, Geller could end up making little money, or even taking a loss. That Neda Fourman made it to age eighty-nine probably was costing Geller a bundle. So … guess what's the only way to assure a profit?"

"I don't need to guess," Rebecca said, disgusted with all she was hearing.

He nodded. "And that, Inspector, is where you come in."

"Would you do a search for Candace Carter?" Rebecca asked Shay. "She may be his latest victim."

As Rebecca logged in to her system at work to get Candace's vital statistics for Shay's search, Richie ordered Chinese from his favorite takeout place, offering a big tip for a super-speedy delivery.

Shay easily found information on Candace Carter. She had a life insurance policy from the school district where she worked. The beneficiary was Lucian Tully.

They had just finished going over the policy on Candace when the doorbell rang. Rebecca went out to the door past the breezeway. She was surprised Richie thought he needed to go with her until she saw the amount of food he'd ordered. He paid, then carried the box filled with goodies.

"All that?"

"I'm hungry. Plus, I like variety. And you know leftover Chinese keeps a few days in the fridge. It makes a great late-night snack."

The implication of his statement hung in the air as she followed him back into the apartment.

oOo

That Shay hardly ate anything when he was with other people was one of the many strange things about him, in Rebecca's opinion. Tonight was no different, and he left the apartment before Rebecca or Richie were half-way through their meals.

Richie always had a good appetite, as did she. He wasn't afraid of ordering adventurous dishes off a Chinese menu, and she was finding each one better than the last. Between food and conversation, she had always found him to be a great dinner companion, which frankly surprised her. Many of the men she chose to date began to bore her after a while. She wondered if the fault was theirs, or if she simply chose the wrong men to date. She knew she'd never choose to date Richie, so why she ended up spending so much time with him was quite baffling.

When they ate their fill, he even helped her move the leftovers into plastic containers to keep better in the refrigerator.

She wondered what she was going to do with him once they were done. Stay? Leave? Go to Big Caesar's? And if it seemed he wanted to stay in her apartment …

They soon finished cleaning up the kitchen. Rebecca looked at him, not sure what to do.

"Since there's nothing more we can do tonight, how about a movie?" he suggested.

"Here? On TV?"

"No, big screen. There's a brand new Captain America film out. Just started yesterday. I've been wanting to see it."

"You like the comic book movies, do you?" she said with a smile.

"What, you think I go for chick flicks?"

"Definitely not." Getting him out of her apartment sounded like a good idea. They checked the movie schedule and were about to head out the door when Richie's phone made an odd chiming sound.

He frowned. "I've got to take this," he said.

He walked away from her as he answered the call. He rarely took a call when he was with her. His phone buzzed a lot, and most of the time he barely glanced at it. This time, even the ring was strange.

She did her best to listen in, but he only said a few "yeahs" and "uh huhs." He looked at her a couple of times, then frowned, and she couldn't help but wonder if the call had to do with the situation that interested the FBI. "Okay. I'll get someone over there right away."

He closed the connection. With the phone still in hand, he said, "I've got to try to catch Shay before he gets home. He'll need to come back this way to pick up something."

"Wait," she said as he was about to call. "If whatever it is, is nearby, we've got a whole hour before the next movie starts. If you want to pick it up yourself, I don't mind waiting."

He checked his watch. "That would be easiest. I'm not sure, though …"

She decided to press him. "Is it one of your clients? You said there was nothing illegal going on. If that's true, what's the problem?"

"That *is* true." He sounded indignant. "Okay. Why not? You're right. No problem."

They drove up to the top of Nob Hill, and then west to a block with a some very attractive older homes and flats. "This is it," he said. As usual in this part of the city, all the street parking was filled, so he parked in front of a driveway. And he wasn't the only one. "Wait here," he said, leaving the keys in the car. "If you see a cop giving tickets, just go around the block until I come back."

"That's tempting." Her hand lightly stroked the wrapped leather steering wheel, and then the top and sides of the leather-covered shift knob.

He took a deep breath before saying, "See how much I trust you?" He didn't wait for a response, but got out of the car and sprinted across the street.

His words made her feel suddenly guilty. He

talked about trusting her, and she was here because the FBI expected her to spy on him. She decided she wouldn't do it. She'd tell Richie the FBI had asked her to report on him and his deals, and she'd tell Brandon Seymour she refused to take part in any of this.

Somehow, she could see both men having a major eruption over such words. Well, too bad.

She shifted so she was leaning against the door to more easily watch the beige building Richie had entered.

Maybe she should take the Porsche for a spin, she thought. She'd probably never get another chance after admitting to Richie she was supposed to spy on him for the FBI and had been tempted to do so.

She turned to see if anyone giving parking tickets was in the area when, instead, she saw two men on the opposite side of the street walking in the direction of the beige building. Something about them, something not right, caught her attention.

She might not have the people skills that Richie had, but she did have a cop's sense for danger and bad guys, and that sense was now on high alert. Those guys surely had nothing to do with Richie—that would be a weird coincidence— but she watched them nonetheless, glad she had her gun in her handbag.

She reached for it now as they slowed down not far from her. She couldn't see anything about them in the dark street, only that they didn't have the jaunty, light movements of teenagers.

They stopped at the same beige building Richie went into. So coincidences do happen. A few steps led from the sidewalk up to a covered entryway. From the car, she couldn't see the actual doorway to know if it was open or shut, or when Richie was leaving his client's home.

Taking care not to let the car door make any noise, Rebecca got out of the Porsche, taking the keys with her. She swung the door closed but didn't even let it latch so as not to alert the two skulkers. She stooped behind the car and waited to be sure they hadn't heard her.

As a muni bus drove down the street, she used it to shelter her as she darted closer to the beige building, and then ducked behind a minivan.

Now, the two sneaks stood with one on each side of the entry, and waited.

She held her gun. A door banged shut and then Richie stepped onto the sidewalk, a flat box tucked under his arm.

The would-be robbers sprang in front of him, both brandishing handguns. "Hand it over," one ordered.

"Easy, guys," Richie said. "This isn't worth getting killed over."

One of them laughed. "Who's going to kill us? You? I don't think so."

"No—the cops who are watching."

Now both laughed. "Yeah, ri—"

"Police! Drop your weapons!" Rebecca shouted from behind the van.

The men both glanced in the direction of her voice and then sped off in the opposite direction.

Richie backed up and leaned against the building, one hand over his heart, the other still clutching the box.

She ran to him. "You all right?"

"Nothing a stiff shot of bourbon won't cure. I hate guns when they're pointed at me."

She breathed a sigh of relief. "Come on," she said. "I think we don't want to go to the movies. We want to go back to my place to see what's so interesting that those guys were ready to kill for it."

Chapter 16

How did you know those men weren't going to shoot you and try a standoff with the police?" Rebecca asked as she got into Richie's car. If they decided to fight it out, it might have turned ugly."

Richie didn't want to think about it. He started the engine. "Too many questions when my heart's still in overdrive."

"Just one then, how did you know I wasn't still sitting down the street in the Porsche?"

"Maybe I had faith in you," he answered.

"Blind faith," she said with a shake of the head.

"Not really."

He mainly had faith that she'd been watching and listening. In fact, he'd been stunned to hear her voice so close, and that her reaction was so quick. Thank God!

They returned to her apartment. Fortunately, she did have bourbon, and he did need it. His hands were still shaking from those two morons holding a gun on him.

He drank his glass down in one gulp and was surprised to see her do the same. He realized she, too, had been shaken up seeing guns drawn.

He sat on the sofa, and she sat beside him.

"So," she said, pointing at the brown-paper wrapped box on her coffee table, "what is it?"

Her breathing sounded back to normal. His might have returned as well except that she was so close. "The box is actually a wooden crate. Inside, carefully packaged so it isn't harmed in any way, is an Assyrian relief on alabaster from about eight-hundred B.C."

The box was about a foot and a half square, and four inches tall. "Sounds valuable."

"Extremely. Mainly because almost all of these reliefs are now in museums. It's almost impossible for a private collector to get one. One was sold at auction a few years back for over eleven million dollars. This one is 'only' worth about two-hundred grand."

"My God! Definitely, don't open it."

Richie saw that she was surprised by the price, but nothing else. That had to mean the FBI agent who'd been watching Claire Baxter was very likely watching him as well. Seeing Rebecca with him, he probably approached her. He wondered how much they had already told her.

"Why did your client give it to you tonight?" Rebecca asked.

"My client's an art dealer. Claire Baxter. But I suspect you know that." She lifted her eyebrows in surprise, but he continued. "Claire is well known in the business—a sterling reputation for only having the highest quality pieces with no questions ever about their authenticity or anything else."

"Claire is the red-haired woman I once saw next to your car?"

"She is noticeable that way," he said. "It all started some two or three weeks ago. She called asking me to check out a new art dealer, an Iraqi, who had some antique pieces for sale. Claire is big with the Silicon Valley crowd who want to invest their money in tangible things that should increase in value—art and antiques, especially museum quality pieces. And they don't care if they're overpaying if they find something they really want."

"I've heard that about them," Rebecca said.

"I had a guy I know look into the dealer. He didn't like what I saw. The dealer's paperwork was incomplete. I suggested Claire back off. She chose to believe the Iraqi when he said he couldn't get more information from a war-torn country. His argument was plausible, but my source still nixed him. The dealer offered Claire a twenty-percent commission, and that was that."

"Money talks, as usual," Rebecca said.

"Exactly. So Claire was working on sales of three pieces of gold jewelry at over fifty grand each, when the FBI came to call, saying the items she sold were stolen from a museum in Baghdad. She freaked and came looking for me. Shay told her I was at some Geary Street theater and apparently she drove to each one looking for my car. But when she saw you, she split."

"She's got a mess on her hands," Rebecca said. "And I guess the FBI confiscated the pieces she was trying to sell."

"Oh, yes," Richie said. "Which means the smugglers want *her* to pay for them. But that's the least of her problems. The FBI wants her to help them capture the man she's been in contact with. But she knows that if the Iraqi, or whatever he is, gets wind of her working with them, he'll kill her. She tried to tell the FBI she wants no part of them, but the agent said she's their best lead, and if she won't help, she'll be charged as an accessory and put in prison."

"So she's between a rock and a hard place," Rebecca said. "Given that, I'd rather take my chances working with the FBI and hoping they'll protect me."

"I agree. I told her to have nothing more to do with the Iraqi. What little I could find tells me the person she's working with is a front man for an entire smuggling ring. The situation is too volatile for her to face alone. I told her I'd talk to the man in charge and find out what they want to make them leave her alone, but keep her out of Federal prison."

"But doing that puts you in danger."

He simply nodded.

She realized that in his explanation of how he made his money, he left out one very important detail—his work easily put him in danger. He wasn't breaking the law, but along its edges were many not so nice people who could turn deadly in an instant.

"It stinks, Richie," she said finally. "Do you have any idea who the two men were waiting for you outside her home?"

"One way to find out." He picked up his cell phone and called Claire Baxter's number. The phone rang, then went to message. "It's Richie. Call me."

He put the phone on the coffee table, and stared at it, expecting her to call back right away.

"Want more bourbon or coffee or food?" Rebecca asked, then with a smirk added, "I've got a lot of left-over Chinese."

"No, nothing. Thanks."

Five minutes later, he called again with the same result. "It makes no sense that she isn't answering or calling. I know she was expecting to hear from me." Richie stood. "I'm going back to her house."

Rebecca put on her jacket and joined him. "Let's go."

It only took a few minutes to reach Claire's

condo. Richie rang the doorbell, and when he received no answer, he turned the doorknob. To his surprise, the door opened.

"Claire?" Richie said as he started up the stairs.

"Wait!" Rebecca took her firearm from her handbag and motioned for Richie to get behind her. One glance at her weapon reminded him of the two men waiting for him the last time he'd been here. He nodded and did as she wanted. If he lived somewhere other than San Francisco, he might be able to get a concealed carry permit and not have to hide behind Rebecca, which he hated. Here, however, hen's teeth were more common than concealed carry permits for private citizens.

As quietly as possible, they went up to Claire's living quarters.

The top of the stairs opened onto the living room. It looked as if some sort of struggle had taken place—a couple of chairs and tables were sitting in awkward positions as if they'd been shoved around. But also, several places on the walls that once held paintings no longer did, and large empty areas gaped on the display shelves.

Rebecca faced him, her expression questioning. He shook his head.

She led the way as they searched the dining room, kitchen, bath and two bedrooms. Claire Baxter wasn't in any of them.

They returned to the living room, and Rebecca put her gun back into her handbag. "I imagine those walls and shelves weren't bare when you were here earlier?"

"The room looked like a showplace," Richie said. "Beautiful furniture and art. This is a real shame."

"I wonder if Baxter ran when whoever robbed her came in."

Richie took out his cell phone and punched in a number. A phone rang in the room. His heart sank. They found Claire's phone under the sofa.

"Don't touch it," Rebecca said. "It might have the fingerprints of the robbers—and likely kidnappers."

Richie used tongs from the kitchen to pick up the phone and then put it in a baggie. "What are you doing?" Rebecca asked.

"Giving it to Shay. He'll be able to find out

who she's been talking to. It could help us find her."

"You can't do that! There might be some vital evidence for the police. I'm calling this in."

He put his hand over her phone. "Calling it in to who? We don't know that anything happened to her. Plus, she's an adult which means there's some sort of waiting period before she's officially missing."

"But you said her home has been burglarized, the furniture knocked around."

He stared at her. "Did I? Hmm. I don't remember that. For all I know, she's messy, and she might have taken her things to sell them. Buying and selling art—that's her business."

"What if something happens to her while you're playing games?" Rebecca cried. "What if she's killed?"

"The fastest way to get her killed is to have the police start snooping around. Besides, isn't the FBI watching her? They might already know where she is."

"Richie—"

He walked down the stairs. "I'm going to find

Shay. Get him started right away. And I'll get Vito to keep an eye on this place in case someone comes back."

She followed.

They reached the sidewalk. "But first I'm going to drop you off back at your apartment."

She frowned. "Not on your life."

"I don't know where this is going to lead, but I do know it's not the sort of thing for you to even know about, let alone take part in. So, yes, you're going home."

She opened her mouth to complain, but then shut it and got into his car.

They both knew he was right.

Chapter 17

The next morning, Rebecca showed Lt. Eastwood a copy of Candace Carter's twenty-thousand dollar life insurance policy in which she made Lucian Tully her beneficiary. Given that, Eastwood approved an autopsy on Carter. Medical examiner Evelyn Ramirez agreed to perform it immediately.

She contacted Rebecca that same afternoon.

"Good instincts, Rebecca!" Ramirez said. Rebecca had never heard her so cheerful. "You were right to be suspicious. Candace Carter was killed by batrachotoxin poisoning. Without your insistence, I doubt anyone would have found it. It's a neurotoxin, but it also has a terrible effect on the heart muscles. Basically, it interferes with a person's heart conduction, causing arrhythmias, extrasystoles, ventricular fibrillation, and other changes which lead to cardiac arrest."

"Does this mean that if someone already has a heart condition, chances of the poison ever being found would be close to impossible?"

"Right. It mimics a heart attack, so no one would bother to look further when dealing with a person with a heart condition, or even in a high risk age group. And it's rare, making it even harder to detect. It's produced by what laymen call a 'poison dart' frog whose habitat is in the warm, high humidity regions of Central and South America. Interestingly, the frog doesn't produce the batrachotoxin itself, but it comes from eating ants or other insects that probably get it from eating a plant we haven't yet identified. Certain beetles also carry the toxin."

For some strange reason, Evelyn assumed Rebecca shared her enthusiasm for details about the weird poison. Rebecca was glad they were talking by phone so Evelyn couldn't see her eyes glaze over as she spouted details and ten-syllable long names. But Rebecca didn't interrupt Evelyn. They were friends and anything that made cutting up dead bodies interesting or in any way enjoyable was okay in Rebecca's book. And she also hoped Evelyn would look upon her strange requests a bit more kindly in the future.

"The way it works," Evelyn continued, "is that when one of these frogs is agitated, feels threatened, or is in pain, the toxin is reflexively released through its skin. They say the Chocó Indians in Columbia first impale a frog on a piece of wood and then roast it alive over a fire. Bubbles of poison form as the frog's skin begins to blister. The Indians prepare their dart tips by touching them to the toxin. Poison darts are enough to drop monkeys and birds in their tracks. When enough toxin is used, nerve paralysis is almost instantaneous. With lesser doses, as in the case of Candace Carter, the heart muscle gives out first."

The description of torturing little innocent frogs was quite enough for Rebecca. She used to play with them when she was a kid in Idaho. She thanked Evelyn and was about to hang up when Evelyn stopped her. "One bit of information to keep in mind," Evelyn said. "This poison is so toxic a medium-size man can be killed with the equivalent of two grains of table salt. It's fifteen times more potent than curare, a more common arrow poison, and ten times more potent than tetrodotoxin found in puffer fish. If someone out there has a supply of this poison, you've got to find it, Rebecca. You've got to find it and stop him."

Hearing that, Rebecca first went to Lt. Eastwood with the news and requested that Neda Fourman's body be exhumed and autopsied immediately, and then, to find out more about Betty Faroni, the woman she'd been close to who also died suddenly, as well as the as-yet-unnamed-Sandorista who died a pauper, Rebecca telephoned Richie's mother.

o0o

"This is my friend, Geraldine Vaccarino," Carmela said. "Geri, this is Inspector Rebecca Mayfield, a friend of Richie's."

When Rebecca called Carmela saying she'd like to talk to her and Geri about the Sandy Geller situation, Carmela invited her to her home. Rebecca had been there once before, during an awkward interlude with Richie. But then, she thought, when wasn't being with Richie awkward for one reason or another?

Geri was waiting when Rebecca arrived.

"I know you're investigating Sandy," Geri said, then pursed her lips. "And I'd like to hate him for my sister's sake, but to tell the truth, I think he's a good man with a good heart. We don't understand what's going on with him. Nothing makes sense, so I really don't want to talk about him."

"I understand, Mrs., uh, Geri," Rebecca said. "But it's up to the police, not you, to determine what's going on. I simply need you to answer a few questions."

Geri looked at Carmela. "What, am I talking to a wall here? Didn't she understand what I said?"

"Help the girl, Geri. For Richie."

For Richie? Rebecca's mouth suddenly felt dry. "I understand your sister, Betty, went to Sandy Geller's séances, and that led to your going to them as well," Rebecca began as she faced Geri. "I've heard she may have spent a lot of money on Geller. Is that true?"

"I don't like this," Geri whispered again, very loudly, to Carmela. "I feel like a double-crosser."

Rebecca couldn't help but sympathize with the feeling.

Carmela glanced at Rebecca. "Geri's very stubborn." Then she leaned closer to her friend. "I know you're no snitch. But you need to help the girl. What if she loses her job if she doesn't get answers? I don't want Richie dating any more women who don't have jobs. They take advantage of him. He's got a good heart, my son. Anyway, it's a simple question."

Rebecca clenched her jaw. She didn't know how much more of Carmela she could take, but then she put what she hoped was a pleasant smile on her face, and waited.

Geri grimaced. "I checked out Sandy Geller because of my sister, god rest her soul. It's true that she gave him all her money. Carmela and I went to a couple of his shows, and afterward, I asked about his séances. A young lady took down information about me, and a week later, I was called in to be interviewed by Sandy himself. The next day, I learned I was accepted. Then, the more I went to see Sandy, the more I saw he was all right. It was my sister who was stupid about taking care of her own money."

Rebecca was surprised to hear that. "Does this mean all is forgiven with Sandy?"

Geri glanced at Carmela before speaking.

"Last month, as I left the séance, I said I had no more money and probably couldn't go to any more of them. Two days later, Lucian Tully came to visit me. He said the Sandoristas had a kind of 'scholarship' fund for people who couldn't afford the séances and asked if I'd like to apply for it. A scholarship, at my age? I wanted to laugh, but I went ahead."

Geri proceeded to tell her the story Richie had already recounted about putting Lucian on as beneficiary to her life insurance policy in exchange for a monthly stipend.

"It's an interesting scheme," Rebecca said when Geri finished. Her thoughts went to fraud, but she doubted many prosecutors would touch the case. It sounded more like a civil suit, if anything since, apparently, no one was coerced into making Lucian their beneficiary.

"But is it a scheme?" Geri asked. "He didn't force me to do anything. Same with Betty, I suspect."

Rebecca didn't tell Geri there was a distinct possibility that her sister had been murdered. If so, 'scheme' was too mild a word for what was going on here. "I understand your sister, Betty, had a lady friend who had gone to Geller and then suddenly died. Do you have her name?"

Geri squared her shoulders, her mouth pinched. "I've heard there was such a woman. I have no idea who she was. Betty and I weren't close."

"I see," Rebecca murmured. She tried a different approach, including Carmela in her next question. "I also heard that both of you attended the funeral of another woman who often attended the séances. Someone who should have had money, but seemed to have lost it all. Can you tell me her name?"

"Oh, yes," Geri said. "That was … hmm. What was her name, Carmela?"

"It's on the tip of my tongue," Carmela said. "Nancy? No, I don't think that's right."

"No. Definitely not Nancy." Geri pursed her lips. "I'd remember if it was Nancy."

"Yes, poor thing. First most of her money was gone, and then she started getting a bit forgetful," Carmela said to Rebecca.

"Yes, such a shame," Geri added with a firm

nod. "What was her name?"

"I can't remember either," Carmela said.

Rebecca looked from one to the other. "If you remember, give me a call." She thanked them for their time and said she needed to be on her way.

Carmela walked her to the door. "So," she said, "I heard you have a new boyfriend."

"Me?" Rebecca was surprised at the statement.

"Don't worry about hurting Richie's feelings," Carmela said. "I don't know if he'll ever settle down."

"Right," Rebecca murmured.

"Women have a biological clock running—if they ever want to have kids at any rate. Not so with men. Sometimes it's not fair."

Rebecca gaped. Where in God's name is all this coming from?

"Richie would make a good father, but sometimes I suspect he'll just wait to be reunited with his fiancée in the next life—she was a saint, that girl, too good for this world. She was perfect for him—and she knew how to cook all his favorites. *Manicotti, saltimbocca, grispedi.* You know?"

Rebecca shook her head.

"No, I guess you don't. Oh, well. No matter. I'm glad to hear you have someone new in your life. It makes it easier. So, you take the information you got from Geri, and you do good with it, okay?"

"I'll try."

"Bene." With a quick goodbye, Carmela shut the door on her.

Chapter 18

Rebecca thought she would hear from Richie immediately after meeting with Carmela and Geri. She even imagined him storming into Homicide to complain about her questioning his precious mother. But he didn't.

She heard nothing at all.

Now, at home, as she ate leftover Chinese food by herself, she realized she felt disappointed.

Okay, that did it. Enough was enough.

Whenever she and Richie were together, she knew his words as well as her own about not wanting anything to do with each other beyond friendship, simply weren't true. Not that she thought he was seriously falling for her, or God forbid, her with him, but she couldn't remember the last time she'd felt such a "zing" when a man simply touched her—or gave her a quick kiss while standing on a sidewalk.

Lust.

That summed up exactly what she felt for him.

Nothing more.

Yesterday, poor, sweet Ray Torres had asked her for a date Saturday night. She realized that would be like going from a Ruth Chris Steakhouse to Chuck E. Cheese. And yes, she hated herself for feeling that way even as she said, "No."

Looking at the situation with Richie logically, the only reason he was still on her mind was because nothing sexual—like making love—had ever happened between them. The last time she'd been in his house, they'd come close. He'd kissed her. And not only had she kissed him back, but immediately knew she wanted lots more than kisses from him. The poor fellow had just been stitched up and was on pain medication from having been shot in the arm, but none of that mattered to her— and from his reaction, it hadn't to him either.

She had no doubt where that kiss would have led if Carmela hadn't taken that moment to swoop in on them like Florence Nightingale, vowing to care for Richie until he was back to normal.

Rebecca suspected that if she had treated Richie the way she had other men she'd been attracted to over the years, he'd be out of her life.

He would have disappointed, bored, or otherwise irritated her, and she'd have dumped him every bit as fast as she had the others.

The best way to deal with this situation now was head-on. And so she would. That very evening.

She phoned Bo Benson and asked if he'd cover for her that night since she was supposed to be on-call. He agreed since she'd taken three of his night shifts recently and he owed her. Besides, no one was murdered on a Tuesday night (usually), so it should be easy for him.

She then changed into an attractive, but casual dress—again with the nylons which meant she was seriously lusting after the man—and headed for Richie's nightclub.

The interesting thing about Big Caesar's was that, while the main part of it was a posh nightclub with a live band and singers, its large bar area was fast gaining the reputation of an upscale place for well-heeled, age thirty and up singles to meet. But she wasn't there to meet someone new. She went there to see one person only. Mr. Big Caesar himself.

As she walked in, the band was playing Big

Bad Voodoo Daddy's "Mr. Pinstripe Suit." Recent jazz and swing tunes as well as the old classics were played at Big Caesar's, and seemed equally popular with all age groups.

She took a stool at the bar and ordered a mai tai. A nice looking but persistent fellow came by to talk to her. She was doing her best to ignore him when Richie showed up. "This is a surprise," he said. The look he gave the stranger caused him to quickly slink away.

For some reason, Richie didn't look or sound happy to see her there. She wondered if she'd read him wrong until she met his eyes. *Naw.* "Just wondering what's happening with your client. I haven't heard from you."

"It's being worked on," he said. "Not a police matter."

A police matter? He might have thought that put her in her place, but not so fast. "I had an interesting conversation with your mother and Geri earlier."

"So I heard."

"Why am I not surprised? Anyway, I think she's worried about 'us' because she mentioned how highly she thought of your fiancée, and made it clear I'd never measure up."

He had the decency to look embarrassed. "I didn't know."

"Maybe you should let her know she has no worries on that score."

He studied her a moment as if trying to figure out where she was going with all this. "I've tried."

"Good," she said. "I must say, I'm surprised any woman interested in you ever got Carmela's blessing. I wonder how she did it."

He thought a moment, then shrugged. "She died."

Rebecca's mouth dropped open. But then, the more she got to know the Amalfis, the more sense his answer made.

He said nothing more about it.

All of a sudden, she felt bad about her bitchy mood, about her reaction to his mother, even about his fiancée. Not only had she put her foot in it, she put both feet in. The band started playing "It Had to be You."

"One of my favorite old songs," she said softly, hoping he saw the apology in her eyes.

He nodded, but made no move to ask her to dance, not even to make small talk. And he loved to talk.

Okay, she'd officially blown it. Bringing up his fiancée, what had she been thinking? Coming here was one of her dumber moves ever. "I should get going."

That seemed to jar him. "Wait. I'm sorry—a lot's on my mind."

"It's okay—"

"Let's get a table. We've got some great shrimp cocktail tonight. Very fresh. And oysters." He lifted an eyebrow. "You know what they say about oysters."

She couldn't deal with him, not after her blunders. She swiveled on the barstool, ready to get off it and leave—to get away and try hard to forget about him. "I've got a date. He won't need any help."

"That's for sure," he said, stepping in front of her. "But if you can tear yourself away from that date, you might want to go along with me to see what Shay found on Claire's phone. I'm meeting him at ten tonight. As I said, it's not a police matter, but if you're interested ..."

Damn. She was. "Let me make a phone call."

"Send a text," he said. "It's faster. Easier."

She took out her phone and texted herself, then put her cell phone away. "All done," she said, a bit too brightly, hoping he hadn't seen through her ruse.

The band, with an alto sax taking the slow, wailing lead, began to play "Embraceable You." Richie didn't need to ask. He took her hand, and they went out on the dance floor. It felt almost too good to be in his arms once more, and the closer she got to him, the better it felt. Afterward, they talked, laughed, ate—including oysters—and drank tonic with lime. Once again Rebecca found, to her dismay, how much she enjoyed simply hanging with Richie. But then it was time to go and meet Shay.

o0o

After leaving Rebecca's car back at her apartment, Richie drove them both to meet with Shay. As they neared the ritzy Presidio Heights area of the city, with huge mansions that had survived the city's devastating 1906 earthquake and fire, she wondered if Shay lived in one of them. If she thought she'd see his home, she was wrong. They met at a restaurant near Arguello.

Shay was already waiting when they arrived. The place was practically empty, and booths offered privacy.

He had a list of phone calls to and from Claire. Several were suspect, and five were from burner phones. One of his skills was to trace the untraceable, but these phones were worse than most. The difficulty only caused Shay to double his efforts.

Finally, he cracked one number and tracked it to a lawyer in San Francisco.

"A shyster." Richie grumbled. "That, we do not need. Let's hope he has nothing to do with any of this."

"Except that his phone call to Claire came Sunday evening, five minutes before two other burner phone calls to her."

"Who's called her since Sunday?" Richie asked.

"No burners. Only the FBI, Brandon Seymour. The only other calls were from old clients, clearly not having anything to do with art smugglers."

Richie nodded, then turned to Rebecca. "Maybe it's time to let Seymour know you can't find Claire Baxter, and neither can I."

Her cheeks reddened, giving away, as if she hadn't already, that Seymour asked her to spy on Richie. "Do you think I'd tell him anything?"

"Yes, I do—if you thought it was necessary. He shows up to talk to you often enough. I can't think of any other reason for his visits. Well, actually I can, but not one that's work related. Also, your face when I told you I was going to Claire Baxter's house told me I was right. You've really got to learn not to give away so much in your expressions."

"My expressions are just fine. But I told Bran"—she knew that could irk him and *his* expression proved she was right—"that he was quite wrong about you being involved in all this."

"Did he believe you?"

"Probably not. And there goes my chance of ever transferring to the FBI."

"Good," he said. A lock of her hair had slid forward almost to her eye, and he gently tucked it behind her ear. "I cause you a bit of trouble, don't I?"

"Yes, you do," she said a lot more emphatically than she meant to.

Shay stood. "I'll see what's going on with the lawyer and put a guy on to watch him. Also, Vito reports nothing at all going on at Baxter's home. Maybe he should give up on it."

Richie agreed. "Move Vito to the lawyer if that makes more sense. And let me know if you crack any more of those burner phones."

"Will do. See you both," Shay said, giving Rebecca what she figured was as close as he ever came to a smile.

Richie drove Rebecca back to her apartment. She looked forward to inviting him inside—just the two of them. Finally. But as soon as he turned into the alley, everything changed.

"FBI," she said, seeing the black van in front of her building. "I'll talk to them."

She got out of the car.

"Stop!" Brandon Seymour yelled as he ran towards them.

No sooner had she shut the car door than

Richie backed out of Mulford and took off.

"Damn it to hell!" Seymour stopped and glared at Rebecca.

"Don't you swear at me! What the hell are you doing here, anyway?" she demanded. "And before you ask, no, I haven't learned anything new."

"You're lying. You were at Claire Baxter's home last night," he roared. "What did she tell you?"

She gawked at him. "You mean you don't know?"

"No! I …" Then he stopped at looked at her. His voice turned quiet. "Don't know what?

"She wasn't there. She's missing."

"What are you talking about?"

"It looked to me like a struggle and abduction, but I can't be sure. How can you not know that? I thought your men were watching her."

"Goddammit!" He got on his cell phone and walked back to his SUV.

Rebecca watched him drive off. As she stepped into the breezeway—alone—she shared his sentiments exactly.

Chapter 19

The next morning, Evelyn Ramirez presented the results of Neda Fourman's postmortem to Rebecca. With no relatives to object, it took no time to obtain needed approvals to dig up the body. Evelyn was so curious about what she might find, she performed the autopsy during the night.

She was over the moon that she now had autopsied two—count them, two—cases of batrachotoxin poisoning. She was even thinking of doing a paper about it.

Rebecca brought evidence of the poisonings and life insurance policies to Lt. Eastwood. She had been working like crazy the past week to find hard proof of Geller's hand in the murders, but so far could find no evidence beyond circumstantial. Although Eastwood had been skeptical of why she was even looking into such a thing, he was now convinced that the two deaths were the tip of a very dangerous iceberg, given the type of poison being used.

He decided she could bring Sandor Geller in for questioning, although she didn't yet have enough evidence to ask for a search warrant of his files. She didn't tell her boss she didn't need a search warrant; she had Shay. She also didn't tell him that, for some reason, she found it hard to believe Sandor Geller was a killer, despite so much pointing towards him. But it wouldn't be the first time a killer had surprised her.

She would lay the facts in front of Geller and see what his explanation was for everything going on. And if she had to lean on him to get his cooperation, so be it.

After quickly briefing Sutter on what she'd been working on, the two of them left for Geller's Octavia Street office.

"I'll drive," Sutter announced. "You're looking awfully tired these days, Rebecca. Usually when homicides are kind of quiet, I use the time to catch up on my sleep. You look like you're doing the exact opposite."

"Guess I've had a lot on my mind lately," she said. Like bodies supposedly dying of natural causes that weren't so natural. Like FBI agents bugging her. And like Richie Amalfi back in her life.

That very morning, as she drove to work listening to the radio, Chris Isaak's "Wicked Game" came on, a song full of warning about feeling desire for the wrong person. Her thoughts had immediately gone to Richie. She had flipped through the dial and stopped when she heard Taylor Swift's "Bad Blood." Now *that* was a song she could relate to.

As much as she wished Bran Seymour hadn't been there to ruin her evening with Richie, if he had come in, she knew where it would have led and she wondered if she wanted her already messed up life to get even worse.

"Rebecca?"

Richie?

"Time to wake up."

Abruptly, she sat up and looked at Sutter. "I wasn't sleeping, just resting my eyes."

"Sure. You weren't snoring either. We've arrived."

"I never ..." But he was already out of the car, and then, so was she.

They walked into Geller's reception room and asked to see him.

"He's not in," the young receptionist said, eying the detectives cautiously since they'd questioned her and the other staff members about Candace Carter. "Can I take a message for him?"

"Is he home?" Rebecca asked.

"I'm not sure. He left at noon and hasn't returned."

"We'll need the address."

"I'm sorry, but Mr. Geller—"

Simultaneously, both inspectors flashed their badges. Without another word, she wrote down Geller's home address.

oOo

Sandy Geller lived in a multi-million dollar condo at the top of Russian Hill, near the apartment Richie's cousin, Angie Amalfi, had lived in before she got married. Rebecca and Sutter walked into the opulent, marble-floor foyer. A suited doorman, middle-aged and balding with a fresh-scrubbed look, greeted them.

Rebecca and Sutter showed their badges and asked for Geller. The doorman buzzed him twice, but received no answer.

"He must not be home," the doorman said.

"Check your logs," Sutter ordered. "I know how your security system works."

Rebecca smirked at Sutter as the doorman did as he was told. She knew Sutter loved to play the tough cop now and then.

"Well, he is home according to our logs of everyone who enters and exits the premises," the befuddled doorman said, staring at the two inspectors. "And his car is in the garage. So I'm afraid he must be indisposed."

"Then get his indisposed ass to answer the door," Sutter demanded. "We don't have all day."

"But if he chooses not to answer, I'm not sure—."

"What if he's sick?" Sutter interrupted. "Or hurt and in desperate need of attention? Do you really want to ignore us and leave him there, possibly bleeding, maybe dying? When would you open the door in that case? After someone complains of the stink, or wonders why bloated flies are pouring out of his apartment vents?"

The doorman swallowed hard. He put in a call

to the building manager and explained the situation. "Yes, sir," he said, then hung up and faced the inspectors. "This way, please."

oOo

Rebecca sensed something was wrong from the moment the doorman stood in front of Geller's apartment and knocked. Not that she believed in ESP, but cops quickly developed a sense of what was going on around them. It helped keep them alive.

Finally, the doorman gave up and used his key to unlock the door.

Rebecca and Sutter entered. As opposed to the rococo style of the building's foyer, Geller's apartment was completely modern, all in grays and browns with crisp lines. It didn't take them long in the starkly decorated space to find out why Geller didn't answer. He was in the living room, face down in a pool of blood still dripping from the spot where his skull had been bashed in.

Chapter 20

After finding Geller's body, Rebecca called the crime scene unit and the medical examiner, while Sutter requested patrolmen to secure the crime scene.

She was torn about handling the investigation. She and Sutter were the on-call team this week, and as someone who knew the deceased she already had some insight—especially since he had been her prime suspect in two other murders.

On the other hand, it was already known she'd spent personal time with him and even had gone to one of his séances. Maybe that hadn't been one of her finer moments, yet, she told herself, it was good investigative work to follow a lead or a hunch.

She phoned Lt. Eastwood and told him of her concerns. Eastwood realized this case would get a lot of press. Geller might not have been hugely popular, but he did have a following. And him being a psychic would lend to all kinds of quips and nasty headlines: *Psychic Fails to Foresee his*

234 | Joanne Pence

own Murder or *Psychic Finally Gets Answers about the Great Beyond.*

Eastwood decided Rebecca needed to remain on the case, but that Bill Sutter should be its public face.

"I'm the what?" Sutter asked, shocked, when Rebecca gave him the news. She was glad it would be him, not her, facing news cameras.

They spent the rest of the day canvassing Geller's apartment building, asking if anyone had seen or heard anything suspicious. When they learned nothing, they expanded their questions to neighbors, and then asked for footage from the surrounding city streets.

Rebecca showed the doorman a photo of Lucian Tully. The doorman recognized him, but hadn't seen him for several days. Although she had initially thought Sandy must have been somehow involved in the ladies' deaths, she now wondered if he wasn't completely innocent. After all, Lucian's name was the one shown as the beneficiary on Neda and Candace's life insurance forms. Was Lucian the one behind everything? Had he fooled her and everyone else so completely?

But then, many people never failed to surprise her—some being a lot worse than she expected, and others, like a certain Richard Joseph Francis Amalfi, surprisingly better. Or so she hoped.

She asked to speak to the building manager, Jim Perkins. He immediately announced he knew nothing because he never spoke with Sandy Geller.

"Never?" That was a surprise to Rebecca.

"No. If he wanted anything, I'd get a call from his secretary," Perkins frowned. "It was made clear to me that all my interaction with him should be in writing. Period."

"I see. Do you recognize this man?" She showed him a photo of Lucian Tully.

"No. I've never seen anyone connected to Geller. I suspect most of his visitors, if any, came in with him through the garage and then took the elevator from there directly up to his floor."

"So anyone entering via the garage would by-pass all security?" she asked.

"Sure. Our tenants deserve some privacy from doormen and cameras. Anyway, a person needs a code to get into the garage, so it's not as if anyone could sneak inside."

"Of course," she said drily, as if no one had ever managed to sneak into a garage with a security code as its doors slowly opened or closed. "Do you have any cameras or security tapes?"

"Certainly. We have four cameras—and tapes. Our system works."

She didn't bother to voice the opinion that a building this size would need a few more than four cameras. "I'd like to see those tapes."

He grimaced with annoyance. "They won't tell you anything we haven't."

"How do you know that?" She gave him a cold stare.

He backed down. "I'll send them to you right away."

o0o

From Geller's building, Rebecca and Sutter went to Lucian's apartment to take him in for questioning. He wasn't there. They talked to his neighbors, but none had any idea about his comings or goings. All said he was quiet, shy, and pleasant, but said little beyond "hello" to any of them.

It wasn't only Lucian, however, who was a suspect. She had nothing to rule out Geller's other employees, clients, and even friends. All were in play until she was able to find something to help narrow the field. And, as yet, that wasn't happening.

Back in Homicide, Rebecca was pleased to find the surveillance tapes from Geller's apartment building had already been delivered.

Sutter gave a brief update to the press, and as soon as it was over, he escaped for home. Rebecca decided to stay, review the tapes, and see what else she could find out.

She was going through exceedingly boring tapes when Brandon Seymour phoned and asked if she had heard anything more about Claire Baxter's disappearance.

"Nope," was her quick reply.

"See what you can get out of Amalfi. He probably knows a lot more than he's said so far."

"Ask him yourself and leave me out of it." How many more ways could she say that to Seymour before he understood she meant it?

"I have no interest in wasting my time trying to get him to cooperate," Seymour said. "You're my best source at the moment. This situation could become dangerous, and I don't want to see you get hurt."

"I can take care of myself," she said tiredly, and hung up.

She went back to the tapes. Now that her prime suspect in Fourman and Carter's deaths was gone, who else would have a motive to kill them and Geller? The three deaths had to be connected.

As expected, the surveillance tapes showed nothing, which meant that whoever went to Geller's condo might have been aware of camera placements—or he let his killer in with him.

Just then her phone rang. It was Seymour again.

"I thought you'd want to know," he began. "We've found Claire Baxter and Amalfi. We're moving in on them."

That jarred her. "Moving in? What do you mean? Where are you?"

o0o

Rebecca rushed down to the docks in the Hunters Point area. It was one of the few areas in the city that hadn't yet gone through the gentrification that was transforming most of San

Francisco. Crime was high; the homes and apartments were mostly small, run down, and covered with bars, boards, and graffiti; and good people did their best to stay off the streets after dark. Near the bay were old piers and warehouses that handled West Coast shipping.

From the appointed meeting place, Seymour led Rebecca to a side street that looked down on a one story building and the empty parking area surrounding it. It was dusk, and a light fog had rolled in. The area was bare of traffic and people, surrounded by a gray mist.

One side of the building had a heavy-looking door with the word "Office" painted on it. The other side had one door and three truck bays with roll-up garage doors. Because of the many parking spaces, they couldn't get any closer to the building without being seen.

"It's a furniture supply warehouse," Seymour said. "Overseas shipments are stored there until retailers come to pick them up. From what we've learned, the front office is fairly small, and most of the building is one big open space filled with furniture crates. We suspect something is going down soon," Seymour said. "My men are in position."

"How do you know Claire Baxter is in there?" Rebecca asked. She didn't like the looks of this at all.

"When we got word of Claire Baxter's disappearance"—Rebecca liked the way he worded that, careful not to admit that *she* was the one who gave the word to Seymour—"I had my men look at any cameras near her apartment, as well as her phone records. We suspect she may be in hot water because of the artifacts we confiscated and now has to pay up. We found she has access to a valuable Assyrian relief that recently was removed from its spot in a local gallery, along with her getting an updated appraisal record about it.

"We also started following Amalfi yesterday and tracking his phone calls as well. We found that first Claire, and now Amalfi, have been calling the same number. Then, late this afternoon, we spotted Amalfi leaving a security vault storage facility— one of those places the rich leave art work too big for a bank—with a box very much the size of the Assyrian relief.

"Tonight, he didn't go to his club. Instead, he headed down here. We suspect arrangements have been made to exchange Claire for the art work. Now, he seems to be waiting. And so are we."

"What are you going to do?" she asked.

"We've got infra-red scanners that show heat signatures for five people in the office. Four keep moving around, and one is still, and the form is such we suspect it's Claire and that she's sitting on one spot, not moving. The people with her are most likely the smugglers Interpol has been tracking. The problem is, they aren't 'mere' smugglers. They're killers. Five in Europe. Also, the Iraqi who alerted Interpol about the Nimrud jewelry being sold in San Francisco was found dead this morning."

"What? Why would they kill him?"

"As a warning to others who might turn to authorities to report wrong-doing."

Rebecca felt a chill run down her back. She wondered if Richie knew the extent of the danger he might be facing.

"We're pretty sure Claire Baxter—and Amalfi—aren't going to make it out of there alive.

Now, we've got to decide if we use hostage negotiators, or simply storm in and do whatever it takes to rescue her."

"But you try to storm the place, they'll all but certainly kill her," she said.

Seymour folded his arms, staring at the warehouse. "We might not have a choice."

Just then, Rebecca's phone vibrated. It was Richie. She walked away from Seymour and answered. "Where are you?" she whispered. "What are you doing?"

"It's about time your friends got here," he said. "I've been freezing my ass off waiting for them."

"Richie, the men who have Claire are killers! You've got to—"

"Just tell Seymour that Claire Baxter is in the warehouse office. Tell him to wait until the action starts, then arrest those mothers."

With that, he hung up.

"Wait! Hello? Hello?"

Seymour turned to see what was going on, and she relayed Richie's message.

"He knew he was followed here?" Seymour said.

"I didn't tell him, if that's what you're thinking," she said hotly.

"What action is he talking about?"

Just then, Richie appeared at the edge of the parking lot. Rebecca smacked Seymour's arm both to get him to be quiet and to watch. They moved a little closer to the warehouse parking lot, taking care to stay huddled next to a building so that it would be difficult for anyone in the warehouse to see them in the fog.

Rebecca watched Richie take a few more steps, then stop and look around. He glanced up towards the area where she and Seymour stood, although she suspected he couldn't actually see them. The realization struck her that if anything went wrong, she might never see him alive again. The thought hurt, even more than she had imagined it would.

She wanted nothing more than to stop him, to tell him to go back to safety and let the FBI handle this. But she knew if she did anything, bullets might fly, and he could easily be the first one killed.

"What the hell is he doing?" Seymour

muttered. He used his mouthpiece to tell his men not to move.

Rebecca's heart was in her throat, and at the moment, all she could do by way of answer was to shake her head.

"Damn!" Seymour said. "He should know better than to trust those guys. He could get Claire Baxter killed. Him, as well. We better stop him."

Rebecca found her voice at that. "No. Let it play out. He knows what he's doing."

"Does he?"

She sure as hell hoped so.

Seymour studied her a moment, his eyes narrow.

Richie began to walk again. In his hands, holding it out in front of him, was the package he had picked up at Claire's home. The Assyrian relief. It was, as the FBI suspected, time for a trade.

Someone opened the warehouse office door and Richie went inside.

Rebecca could scarcely breathe as the minutes ticked by.

"I don't want to wait much longer," Seymour said. "We could warn them that we're here, use hostage negotiators."

"Not yet," she said. "He wouldn't be here alone. His people know what's going on."

"You seem to know a lot about him and his 'people.'"

"Which means you should listen to what I'm telling you." Her voice sounded both harsh and scared, and Seymour again gave her a strange look.

Finally, they saw the office door open. Claire stepped out. Rebecca froze, not even breathing. Where—?

Richie appeared in the doorway and lunged at Claire, knocking her to the ground. At that very moment, a shot rang out, and then all hell broke loose as a barrage of gunfire from the alley opposite the parking lot hit the warehouse walls and broke the leaded window by the office door. People inside the warehouse fired back through the open door and a broken window.

"What the f--!" Seymour yelled and began barking orders at his men through his earpiece.

Richie half-dragged Claire to one side of the warehouse. A Mercedes sped towards them. The back door swung open and Richie pushed Claire into the car and then jumped in after her. As the door was pulled shut, the Mercedes sped away.

"Move in!" Seymour shouted to his people. "Stop that car and surround the warehouse. We're going in!"

The Mercedes sped out of the parking lot. Federal agents in a black SUV raced after it as others ran towards the warehouse. They stopped and took cover as they exchanged gunfire with the warehouse inhabitants.

Then, the shooting from inside the warehouse office stopped, and one of the garage doors on the far side of the building rolled open. A voice shouted that they were giving up.

All went silent as two agents carefully approached the truck bay. Two men soon came out of the building, their hands high in the air.

"I guess you can go down and see what's left in the warehouse," Rebecca said to Seymour.

"Who the hell was doing all that shooting?" Seymour demanded. "Just who are Amalfi's 'people'?"

"I suspect you know as much as I do," she replied.

Seymour fumed. "I'm not so sure about that," he muttered, then took a deep breath. "But right now, come with me and take a look. You know this is an FBI case, but the rest of the SFPD might not agree. Maybe if you're there, we can avoid a jurisdictional fight."

She looked in the direction of the street that the Mercedes with Richie and Claire had fled down, the street the FBI had taken while chasing them. It looked empty, although the fog limited visibility greatly. She could only hope Richie and the others had been able to get away.

"Be assured," she said after a while, "I don't want any part of what went on here just now."

Chapter 21

Despite everything else going on, Rebecca and Sutter remained the on-call team that week, and Rebecca was awakened by a six a.m. call about a dead body in the Ingleside district. It turned out to have been a gang shooting, and although the two homicide inspectors had taken charge of the case, the Gang Task Force quickly arrested the killer. Witnesses and a confession ended the case.

Rebecca was glad of that since she had been in Homicide until midnight the night before, writing a report on the shoot-out in Hunters Point. She stuck to the facts as she saw them: four men, two had died at the scene, the FBI took the other two men into custody, and a number of people—as yet unofficially identified—had fled the scene. Her report made it clear this had been an FBI-led operation, and she had been called in as a courtesy to the SFPD since it took place within the city limits.

She had not heard anything from Richie last

evening or that morning.

Now, although weary, Rebecca knew it would be impossible to go back to sleep if she went home. Instead, she turned to the information pulled from Geller's condo by the crime scene investigators. His autopsy had been scheduled, but not yet performed.

She had just taken a quick look at the report—nothing new jumped out at her—when Brandon Seymour phoned.

"The two warehouse survivors are singing like birds," he said. "Thanks to them, we've already retrieved the five missing pieces of Nimrud jewelry."

"Good news," Rebecca said. She didn't care about the artifacts. "Have you talked to Amalfi or Baxter yet?"

"Not yet. Baxter was given a sedative by her doctor, and her lawyer doesn't want her bothered. He says we have everything wrong, and that she wants no part of anything. Right now, we can arrest her for *trying* to sell illegal artifacts, but the attorney claims the paperwork she was given will prove that she acted in good faith. He asked if we're claiming she should have been suspicious simply because the seller was an Iraqi Muslim, and if so, wasn't that profiling? Did we plan to arrest her because she's not bigoted?

"The bastard even accused me of trying to ruin the lady's reputation as a legitimate art dealer, and said he would do everything possible to keep her far away from us or any investigation. As if I give a rat's ass about her sales creds."

"In other words, she'll get off," Rebecca stated. At Seymour's mumbled 'yeah,' she then asked, "What about Richie?"

Seymour snorted. "Baxter's lawyer claimed he was only there to bring the Middle Eastern artwork to the men with Claire—that they were her clients, and this was a sale, not a kidnapping. He said Claire believes the people shooting at them were rival smugglers or thieves, God only knows. The lawyer claims Amalfi was lucky to get Claire out of there unharmed. That we should be praising him, not wanting to arrest him."

"There are more holes in that story than Swiss cheese," Rebecca said.

"It'll completely shatter once we find the

shooter."

"What does Richie say?"

"We haven't located him yet, or the men with him."

"I see." That wasn't good.

Seymour continued, his frustration evident with every word. "The bullets that killed the two men in the warehouse were from a high-powered semi-automatic rifle, probably an AR-15 or something similar. The shooter was outside the building, supposedly firing blindly, but still managed to hit two men. Despite Claire Baxter's story that the attack came from a rival group of smugglers, we're sure the shooter was one of Amalfi's men. Have you heard of a sharp-shooter among them?"

"Me? How should I know? I was with you, remember? You're the one who told me what was going on."

"I think you have a good idea who was firing that rifle, Mayfield."

So it was "Mayfield" now, she thought. So much for a friendly relationship, which actually had never been all that friendly. She was all but certain

Shay had been the shooter, and could imagine him using an infrared camera, or even better, Richie wearing some sort of camera to let Shay see the inside of the office, Claire, the men involved, who was armed and so on. Shay had the kind of computer brain that could triangulate distances and whatever else he needed to come up with to know where to shoot. She was also certain Shay's first shot had to have been a kill shot. If he had missed, Richie or Claire or both, might be dead now.

But she wasn't about to tell Seymour any of that. "Richie Amalfi doesn't tell me what he's up to, believe me."

"We'll find him and nail him and the shooter to the wall."

She wouldn't have been surprised if Seymour arrested Richie as a ploy to get more information out of him about the shooter. After all, two men had been killed.

"That's pretty gutsy of you," she said.

"Gutsy? To take on Amalfi? I don't think so!" Seymour all but spat the words.

"Not him. This case. You think the media won't have a field day if you tell them the FBI stood around doing nothing while a civilian pulled off a hostage rescue that led to the recovery of valuable art work? Or, even worse, that it was a trigger-happy civilian, probably a former military sniper given the accuracy, who got involved in a shoot-out on a San Francisco street, and the FBI let it happen?"

"It wasn't that way."

"No. I agree, but you know the press. They'll do whatever they can to make the FBI look bad. And that won't help you or anyone else."

There was a long silence. "I really hate this," Seymour admitted. "And the press!"

"I know, but given reality in this city and how ugly things can turn, it might be in the FBI's best interest to walk away. As things now stand, an FBI sting recovered eight pieces of irreplaceable Nimrud jewels, and arrested a deadly smuggling ring. Few will mourn the two dead smugglers. Besides, the press and public are so much more interested in my case—the murdered psychic—that this one can fly under the radar. Unless you want to bring it to their attention."

"No, I definitely don't want to do that."

"It's up to you, of course."

"Damn it! Screw them all!" Seymour shouted, and with that, hung up.

oOo

Rebecca and Sutter returned to Geller's Octavia Street offices that afternoon. The press was all but camped out in front of the beautiful building housing them, and it had become a fixture on local news.

While Sutter gave the reporters a brief statement, Rebecca went inside. The secretary had taken charge and had called everyone in to work. There was a surprising amount of activity going on.

Rebecca went straight to the office of Stan Bendix, the bookkeeper. "I understand Mr. Geller has been sending out payments to a number of his Sandorista clients," she said. "I'd like to see those records."

Stan Bendix was shaped more like a big overstuffed teddy bear than a man. He was pudgy and soft-looking; with long, brown hair; flat, round, brown eyes; puffy cheeks; and a heavy brown sweater. He stood as she entered. "I don't know what you mean," he said with a slight stutter.

"I mean I have proof that eight people—at least—were receiving payments. Surely, you know that." Her eyes narrowed. Shay couldn't have been wrong, could he?

"No payments like that were sent out of this office," he repeated.

"Prove it," she said.

"Now?"

She showed him her search warrant for the facility, then pulled the guest chair to his side so she could look onto the computer screen with him. "Of course, now."

Bendix opened up his files. She didn't really know much about what she was looking at, but had him walk her through the different categories of the Geller account.

Nothing struck her as odd until they reached the Sandorista category. The overall budget for the account showed a yearly income of $48,000, an outgo of $48,000, and a net of $0.

"What's that all about?" she asked.

"The Sandoristas are a great group. I'm one myself. Sandy set up the Sandoristas as a non-profit association for educational purposes. He donates money each year for a scholarship for people who can't afford his fees. This is that category. The members take care of determining how to spend the money—who it should go to and all. Sandy has, had, no part in that."

"So, who did they decide to give scholarships to?" she asked.

Bendix blanched. "You'll have to ask one of the Sandoristas. They don't give me that information."

"They don't? If that's the case, how do you know how much should go into this scholarship category?"

"That's easy. It's been the same amount for the past four years. It started small, but then rose. As I said, Sandy makes his yearly contribution, and that ends our involvement."

"Let me see who's being granted the scholarships," Rebecca said.

"Okay." He opened the Sandorista online bank account. "Hmm. This is strange."

She looked at the computer screen. It showed, each year, a transfer of the entire $48,000 from the Sandorista bank account to a completely different account owned by the Colonial Bank on Noriega Street in San Francisco. "Why there?" she asked.

Now, Bendix's skin was white, his chin quivering. "I have no idea. We always understood the group made donations directly out of the account we set up for them. No one told me about that bank."

"Who does know about it?"

"I'm not sure. The head of the Sandorista club is a woman in New York City, at the moment. She should know."

She claimed she had never accessed the account or had anything to do with it. She had the account's information, but no password. She understood Geller's office—his bookkeeper— handled the scholarships. Bendix was horrified to hear that.

Bendix made a quick phone call to the Bank. Fortunately, the account had been opened under the Sandorista umbrella. He gave his credentials, Rebecca explained the police involvement, and the bank manager gave them access.

"Oh, my," Bendix said.

From the account, $500 per month was

transferred to eight people. Also, every few months, a large amount—tens of thousands of dollars—went into that account. It was withdrawn, in total, one or two days after it arrived.

Rebecca did a quick calculation giving eight people $500 per month would be $48,000 a year. The larger amounts, she suspected, were life insurance payouts when one of them died. It was quickly withdrawn by whoever was behind the scheme. So the question was, who?

"I'll get my computer forensics experts on this," she said, and used a thumb drive to copy the files pertaining to the off-book "scholarship" operation.

She planned to give the information to Shay for him to figure out who was getting into that account to withdraw money.

She left the bookkeeper staring blankly at the screen.

She then went off and found Sutter. He had left the press and was talking to Geller's other employees—secretary, receptionist, advertising and newsletter writers. All were devastated by Sandy's death, and certain that Lucian Tully had nothing to do with it. They believed he might have seen or knew something that made him fear for his own life and had gone into hiding.

Rebecca and Sutter were well aware that some unknown third party could be involved in this tangled web, so Sutter went off to question some disgruntled former clients as potential leads. Rebecca returned to Homicide.

There, she got Lt. Eastwood to issue a BOLO on Lucian, making it clear it was a "be on the lookout" because he was wanted for questioning, not due to an arrest warrant.

She dug into Lucian's background, doing computer searches, but found out little.

She phoned his parents' home in Joplin, Missouri. His mother, Dora Tully, answered. Rebecca quickly explained who she was, and that she was trying to locate Lucian.

"I have no idea where he is," Dora said. "I haven't spoken to him in quite a while."

"No one here seems to know who his friends are, or if he has anyone he's particularly close to. Do you have names of any people we might check with?"

"Lucian never talked to me or his father about friends. In fact, he doesn't talk to us at all, not since we told him he was being ridiculous working for someone who holds séances. I mean, really, what kind of career choice is that?"

Her words made Rebecca curious. "When did you last talk to him?"

"Let's see. He's now twenty-six. It was on his twenty-second birthday. The call ended up being so ugly, we never called him back, and he never phoned us."

"I see," Rebecca said. So much for that lead. She quickly ended the call.

She was trying to think of a way to get a search warrant issued for Lucian's apartment. Maybe the easiest way would be if Shay could find a connection to him on the bank account information she'd gotten from Sandy's accountant. That should help convince a judge to let them search Lucian's apartment. She knew she should go to the CSI unit for that, but her request would have to wait in line—the big murder case Paavo and Yosh had been working on these past few days was taking up most of their time. She could get an answer faster from Shay.

As she reached for her phone to call Richie, she looked up.

Richie strode into Homicide. He didn't look at anyone but her, his face more angry and stricken than Rebecca had ever seen it. She stood.

A lull spread over the bureau, as if not only Rebecca, but also Inspectors Luis Calderon and Bo Benson, the secretary, Elizabeth, and even Lt. Eastwood, seemed to stop what they were doing and watch.

"What is it?" she asked.

"Terrible. Let's go."

"I can't just—"

"You've got to. Take your gun."

"Don't worry about being on-call, Rebecca," Bo Benson told her. "Go."

She looked at him, and then Richie. Nodding thanks to Bo, she grabbed her jacket, badge and firearm and hurried after Richie to the elevator. She could hear Calderon's long, low whistle as she went.

Waiting for the elevator, Richie paced back and forth, his hand rubbing the back of his head.

"What happened?" she asked.

"I'm worried about my mother and maybe her friend Geri."

"Worried? Why?"

"Your boy, Lucian, is involved."

She couldn't imagine ... "Lucian? Are you sure?"

The elevator bonged, and she had to wait until they were in the parking lot and on the way to his Porsche before he answered.

"I'm not sure of anything, only that I got a phone call. I saw it was from Carmela and so I answered. I said hello, but no one spoke. Then I heard someone say 'Stop her, goddammit.' She yelled, 'Lucian, no,' and then the phone went dead."

"My God!"

"Tell me about it." He smacked the roof of his beloved Porsche with his fist. "If that bastard hurts her, I'll kill him. I swear it."

"Don't worry. Carmela will be fine. She's too tough for anything to hurt her. But if she's in danger, I've got to call it in."

"No!"

"No? What do you mean, no?"

They both got into the car and he pealed out of the lot. "My mother's a saint. A saint, I swear it. She'd do anything for me."

"I know." It was amazing, Rebecca thought, with all the 'saints' hanging around Richie that he was so devilish. She didn't know what to make of this. "Richie, look, let me call some guys on the force. They'll help us."

"I said no."

"This is crazy!" She insisted. "That phone call sounded like a kidnapping! If so, we'll need help finding her. And once we do, we'll need back-up."

"Too much could go wrong. We can handle it."

"You're being foolish, and stubborn! Let me call—"

"I said forget it."

He made no sense to her. "Where are we going?"

His jaw was so tight she didn't know how he could speak. "To meet Shay. He's trying to find Carmela right now. I called Geri, no answer. I got hold of her daughter-in-law who lives next door to her. She thought Geri was with Carmela. But no one knows where either woman is."

"Is Shay tracking her cell phone?"

"No. I tried calling her back, but the call didn't go through. I suspect they trashed the SIM card."

"Then how … Wait. Don't tell me you put a tracker on your own mother. You didn't."

"Only in the lining of her favorite wallet. And on her rosary—a tiny one that goes behind the Virgin where the three strands of beads meet." He sped up as the light turned yellow and was in the intersection as it switched to red. "She never goes anywhere without taking at least one of them or her cell phone with her. Hopefully, that son of a bitch didn't take them away from her."

"Whatever possessed you to do such a thing? Were you afraid because of your business—"

"Stop with the business cracks, already," he yelled as he pulled into a parking space—a red zone. "It's rarely dangerous. Most of the time. No, it was because I kept reading about old people wandering off and how the family doesn't recognize the symptoms until it's too late. She seems fine to me, but I'm family."

"She is fine, believe me." She patted his shoulder seeing he was beyond distraught. "And she's not old. When she finds out, you are so dead."

"I know. That's why I can't tell her."

"Although, she might forgive you once she realizes the tracker was used to find her more quickly than the police might have done."

"I doubt it," he said, opening the car door to get out.

She nodded as she did the same. "You're right."

oOo

Richie led Rebecca to a Starbuck's barely a half mile from the Hall of Justice. Shay sat at a back table with his laptop set up.

Shay immediately told Richie he'd found a faint signal from Carmela's tracker, but it seemed to be coming from out in the Pacific. "This makes no sense," Shay said. "Unless Lucian already killed Carmela and Geri and dumped them and their belongings into the ocean."

"I know you're a heartless bastard," Richie said through gritted teeth, "but you ever again even *think* something like that about my mother, let alone say it, you are dead meat."

Shay held up both hands. "Just being real."

"Exactly where is the signal coming from?" Rebecca asked.

"A little south of Half Moon Bay." Shay pointed to the screen.

"I may know where Lucian is," Rebecca said. "It might look like it's in the ocean, but that's because there's a small peninsula out there. It has no roads, no people—nothing has ever been built on it because it's been privately owned for over a century. A bit inland, there's a house said to be haunted. Geller was developing a TV special about it."

Richie frowned. "Why bring Carmela and Geri there?"

Rebecca shook her head, as bewildered as he was.

Shay gave Richie a micro-tablet that included the app tracking his mother's GPS signal. "You can use this to help when you're down there. It should be accurate within a hundred-fifty feet or so."

Richie nodded. "You keep searching. Keep

trying to tap into Lucian's cell phone, or Geri Vaccarino's, and anyone else who might be involved in this mess. My phone is synced to yours, so if this is a kidnapping, and they call me, you'll know about it. Vito should be here soon. Then you and Vito know what to do. Rebecca and I will head for Half Moon Bay after a quick stop to switch to her SUV."

"My car?" Rebecca said. "Why? Yours will be much better on those winding roads of Highway One."

"Yeah, but we'll put that siren thing on your roof and blow through stop signs and everything else."

Rebecca stepped closer to Shay. "Tell him we need to bring in law enforcement. I have a contact in the FBI who, frankly, owes both of us. We can get his help, I'm sure. This is serious. What if you're wrong, Shay? We need to find out exactly what happened."

Shay looked from her to Richie, then back to his computer. He made no reply.

Rebecca straightened, scarcely believing his rebuff.

Just then, Vito entered the coffee shop.

"Hey, Inspector," he said. "Glad to see you back again. Thanks for your help the other night."

Her eyebrows rose. "You were there, too?"

"Who you think drove the Mercedes?" His grin widened. "I left those feds in the dust. It was great."

"Enough, Vito," Richie warned.

Vito's eyes widened, then he clamped his mouth shut and sat down across from Shay.

"Let's go," Richie said to Rebecca.

She looked from Shay, to Vito, to Richie. She didn't agree with what they were doing, but decided it was better to go along than to fight with them. Hopefully, she could stop things from spinning too far afield. And eventually, she *would* call in the authorities.

She gave Shay the thumb drive with the Sandorista financial information, quickly explaining what she needed. Then she turned to Richie. "Ready."

Chapter 22

Rebecca could only hope she was right that Lucian had gone to the Falls Meadow house in Half Moon Bay. She assumed Sandy hadn't told his assistant that he once had brought her out there. Without knowing that, Lucian probably thought it was a perfect hide-out. Isolated, tree and shrub-covered, and the locals were afraid to get too close to it since it was said to be haunted.

Richie asked what she knew of the house in Half Moon Bay, so she gave a quick explanation of the property's layout, and that it was supposedly haunted by the ghost of Astrid Bruckmann.

"I hate ghosts," was his only comment.

The gate was padlocked. It could mean no one was there, or that someone wanted to make it appear no one was there.

She got out and went through the tools she carried in the Explorer's cargo space. Going to strange crime scenes meant a lot of forced entry tools were often needed. She pulled out a bolt

270 | Joanne Pence

cutter.

Richie took it and cut off the lock.

She drove down the path towards the house, and went to the same flat, gravel-filled parking area that Geller had used at the end of the dirt driveway. She saw no other car but the surrounding land was so filled with trees and overgrown brush, a car would be relatively easy to hide.

They got out of the SUV and looked up at the house atop a small bluff. They saw no lights, no movement, and the windows appeared to be covered with drapery.

"Where's Lucian's car?" Richie sounded exasperated and disappointed. "I wonder if we guessed wrong."

"But the GPS tracker tells us they're here somewhere," she said, looking at the micro-tablet. "There are some twenty acres of land. It was once a dairy farm, so there are most likely other buildings on the property."

They walked first to the edge of the hillside above the beach. From there, they could get a good sense of the area's topography. The beach as well as the land around the house and parking area all appeared empty. Too empty.

"Something may have happened over there," Richie said, looking southward. He headed that way.

"Where?"

"Look." He pointed at the ground a bit in front of them. "A lot of the weeds have been smashed down and stalks broken as if something drove over them." He followed the line of disturbed brush, to the top of a cliff, the beach far below.

A car lay at the foot of the cliff. The tide was in, and the front of the car and the entire passenger section were submerged. Only a little of the trunk showed when the tide went out.

"Aw, no," Richie murmured and started searching for a way down. "I've got to get down there."

"Wait." Rebecca grabbed his arm. "There's no way you or anyone else could climb down that."

"I can't just leave them." He continued along the cliff's rim, searching.

"Richie," she said. "If anyone is still inside, it's too late for them."

He sucked in his breath. "Do you know what

272 | Joanne Pence

kind of car Lucian drove?"

She hesitated, then said, "A red Kia."

"It's red," he said, his voice flat. "And small."

The look he gave her was heartbreaking.

"We need to call for help," she said.

He took out his cell phone. It showed no service.

He dropped his arms, shoulders sagged, head bent as he looked down at the water. He watched the waves rush in, cover the car, and then flow back out to sea. "My God."

She put her arm around his back. "We don't know that anyone is in there. Maybe Lucian was trying to hide the car. We just don't know."

His eyes were empty. "Or they're all dead."

"Until it's proven otherwise, I believe they're alive," she whispered. "And so should you."

She could feel a shudder go through his body and turned him away from the ugliness below the cliff. She put her arms around him, her head against his, trying to give both comfort and strength.

"God, Rebecca," he whispered as his arms tightened around her. "I can't—"

"What a sweet scene."

They broke away from each other and turned towards the sound of the voice behind them.

Chapter 23

Coming out of the bushes was the older gray-haired man Richie had met when he went with Rebecca to interview the Sandoristas. "I had hoped you might kill yourselves on that cliff and save me the trouble, but no such luck."

"Henry Highfield," Rebecca said. "What's going on?"

Richie could all but feel her trying to figure out a way to disarm the Sandorista. He wondered if the guy's wife was nearby or if old Henry was going it alone out here.

"First, slowly put your gun on the ground and then kick it over to me."

"I'm not giving you my weapon," she said.

"You will unless you and your boyfriend want to get shot. And if Marta hears shots fired, she just might get nervous and shoot the old ladies in there with her."

Richie silently thanked God that his mother wasn't in the scrap heap now littering the ocean. He remained still, not daring to move in case it would cause Rebecca to act rather than to think through the best way to handle Highfield's threats.

Rebecca slowly pulled her revolver from her waist holster, placed it on the ground, and kicked it towards Highfield. His eyes on her the entire time, he stooped to pick it up and put it in his jacket pocket.

"Good," he said. "Now, get going. Maybe those two old bags will shut up and cooperate when they see you two—or know that if they don't, they'll have to watch you two get tortured, and maybe end up dead."

Richie and Rebecca said nothing as Highfield directed them up to the old house. Richie was surprised that the inside was fully furnished, as if someone still lived there.

As he entered the dining room, the first thing he saw was his mother and Geri seated at a round table. Their frightened eyes and awkward posture told him they were being held with their hands tied behind their backs. Fury surged through him.

Marta also sat at the table, near the back wall. She stood as they entered.

He quickly studied the room—an oak table, chairs and sideboard, striped wallpaper, and over the windows lacy sheers with dark red drapery on each side. A sepia photograph in a wood frame over the sideboard showed an unsmiling family—a husband, wife, and a young daughter. Richie guessed the woman was the one who supposedly now haunted the house.

"*Madonna!* Richie, why did you let him capture you?" Carmela asked.

Good. She's not hurt. Relief surged through him. "Already with the criticism?" His throat felt thick as he spoke. "At least we found you."

"That's supposed to make me feel better?" Carmela frowned, but she couldn't keep up the banter. Her eyes filled with tears. "I wish you hadn't found me. I don't want you hurt. These people, they're crazy."

He couldn't bear seeing her this way. "It'll be okay, Ma. I promise you."

"Why are you doing all this?" Rebecca asked, looking from Henry to Marta who was again sitting. "Why did you snatch these women?"

"They figured it out," he said simply.

"It was actually kind of funny," Marta added. "Sandy, Lucian, and the entire San Francisco Police Department were all running around wondering what was going on, and two old broads from North Beach figured out what was really happening."

"Who's an old broad, you witch!" Carmela sneered at her.

"Is that true, Ma?" Richie asked, impressed.

"All we wanted was to get back Geri's sister's money," Carmela said firmly. "First, we could see that Lucian couldn't scam a flea. He was such a complete innocent he'd do whatever Sandy wanted without question. Or whatever he thought Sandy wanted."

"I don't get it," Richie admitted.

Carmela and Geri smiled smugly at each other. Richie knew they were up to something. "Spirits of some of the women who spent most of their money on Sandy came to us during the séances," Carmela said. "We're quite good at séances, by the way."

"You are?"

"Oh yes. We have a gift."

Geri nodded, and she took over their

explanation. "Spirits came to us and said things that only someone who understood how the insurance scheme worked would understand. That was when we saw that Sandy had no part in it—he didn't have a clue what the spirits were talking about, but Henry and Marta did." She gave Henry and Marta a vicious glare.

Richie felt the Highfield's tension rise with each word Geri spoke.

"The next thing we knew," Carmela said, "poor Sandy was dead, and Lucian was hiding. We don't know why he hid—probably grief, maybe fear. The boy was out there where the buses don't run, you know. Apparently, he called his friends, Henry and Marta, thinking they would help him. They helped him all the way to this house, picking up Geri and me as they went."

"It's all their fault," Marta said to Rebecca. "If they hadn't stuck their noses in, Sandy and Lucian would both still be alive."

"Lucian was in that car?" Richie said, looking a bit ill.

"He got in over his head," Henry said. "Literally."

"You two set up the fake 'scholarship account' didn't you?" Rebecca said. "You had eight other women and men receiving payments they thought were from Sandy. I suspect that means you had life insurance policies on all of them. Policies on which you showed Lucian's name, but when the insured died, you two got the money."

Marta smiled. "The attorney I once worked for was great at estate planning, including insurance." She sounded oddly proud of having learned how to con people.

"No one was hurt," Henry said. "Those people were already close to death."

"What made you so nervous," Rebecca asked, "that you went after Sandy?"

"Sandy himself," Marta answered. "Your questions made him curious. He started his own investigation and quickly turned to the Sandorista scholarship account. It was an account he rarely, if ever, checked on. Why should he? We were long-time, trusted members, so of course we handled it for him."

Henry jumped in. "Sandy wanted to know who was getting the scholarships, and how the money was being used. After we heard Sandy started questioning people, we waited outside his condo for him to get home. We stopped him as he was pulling into his garage, sounding contrite and saying we needed to talk. He had us enter the garage and ride up to his condo with him on the private elevator."

"So no one knew you were there," Rebecca said.

"Marta's Spirit Guide had warned her he was suspicious, even ready to go to you, Rebecca, with his accusations. We had to stop him. And we did."

"So why didn't you stop with Sandy's death?" Rebecca asked.

"Because we'll need money. With Sandy's death, there'd be no more Sandoristas, which meant no more money coming in for us. So we decided to kill two—or more—birds with one stone, so to speak. Get Marta's inheritance, and get rid of everyone who might realize we were behind this, namely, Lucian and 'Thelma and Louise' there."

"What inheritance?" Richie asked.

"The Bruckmann gold. It's hidden here, somewhere. It's ironic that we told Sandy about this place, expecting he would get the ghost to tell him where the gold was hidden. But he couldn't even get her to appear to him—he only *said* he did. And then, he decided to do a TV special about her and the gold. Once that happened, we knew we'd have treasure hunters from all over the country sneaking in to try to find the gold."

"But Sandy said the Bruckmann gold was just a local myth, a fairy tale," Rebecca stated. "People have searched for it for years, and no one has ever found it."

"That's what Sandy thought, but we know it's real." Henry gloated as he announced, "Marta's mother was Inga Bruckmann, the ghost's daughter. Her father, Gunter, did survive the trip out to the sea that day. He wasn't far out from the pier when he saw the skiff start taking in water, and then understood just how crazy his wife was. The only thing he loved about his life in Falls Meadow was his child. He made it ashore and took his daughter away with him. All that's known is that, eventually, they ended up living in Sacramento. The wife went nuts. What a vengeance, don't you think?"

"Supposedly, Gunter told Inga where the gold

was hidden, but by the time Marta learned that the bizarre stories about her family were true, it was too late. Inga had developed dementia. Anyway, when we saw that those two women have a gift that's even stronger than Sandy's. Marta's spirit guide told her what we had to do."

"The energy in this room is wonderful," Marta said. "Two scared older women, a younger man worried about his mother, a woman who's in love with him worried about him. This is exactly what we need."

"You're wrong about one assumption," Rebecca said.

Richie's eyebrows went up. "That's the *only* thing you have to say about all this?"

Rebecca frowned at him.

Henry chortled. "What's happening here reminds me of the poison dart frog and how when they get scared they secrete a poison so deadly it can't be legally transported, but for those of us who have traveled a lot in our youth, you'd be surprised at what we've managed to get our hands on and to bring home."

"I don't care how much you travel," Rebecca

said. "You can't easily transport that kind of poison."

"Who said it was easy? I may have been 'just' a high school science teacher, but each summer I could take two months off to travel around the world with my dear wife. I learned some amazing things over time."

"Enough of all that," Marta said, her patience gone. "It's time for the six of us to hold a séance, to put the energy here to good purpose. Together, we're going to get my grandmother to tell me where the gold is."

"Why would she want to tell you anything?" Carmela asked. "You're a terrible person! A killer! She should strike you dead!"

"I can feel her presence," Marta claimed. "She's waiting to speak to me."

"Waiting to disown you," Carmela muttered.

"Marta, you hold the gun to the mother's head while I tie up these two," Henry said. He had Richie sit on a chair between Carmela and Geri, and situated Rebecca between him and Marta.

He tied their torsos to the back and seat of their chairs, leaving their arms and hands free and then did the same with Carmela and Geri. He needed all of them to be able to hold hands in a circle.

Next, he lit three candles and put them in the center of the table, then shut the door and, since it was only three o'clock in the afternoon, he drew the drapes to make the room as dark as possible for the séance.

He and Marta took their places at the table. "Breathe in, everyone. Focus on the candles, and now breathe out," Henry said. "Breathe slowly. In … out. Focus."

Marta blew out the first candle.

"Take each other's hands," she said, "and be sure not to let go, no matter what happens."

She blew out the second candle. "Shut your eyes and relax," she ordered, in a hushed voice.

Carmela snorted.

"Come, Astrid!" Marta called. "Come to us!"

"You're going to die," Carmela said, "and I don't need spirits to tell me that."

"Come spirit! Astrid Bruckmann, it's me, your granddaughter Marta calling you. I need your help. I need to find the gold. Help me, please."

Nothing happened. Marta leaned forward and

blew out the last candle. The room was now completely black except for a scant amount of light seeping in at the top edge of the heavy red drapes.

Marta repeated her plea. Again, all remained silent.

Richie's eyes slowly adjusted to the dark, and he could make out some images.

Marta called even louder. "We welcome you, Astrid Bruckmann. Give us a sign you're here."

Richie slowly slid his and Carmela's joined hands under the edge of the table top.

"Come, Astrid, Grandmother. Are you here?"

Richie lifted the table ever so slightly, let go, and quickly put their hands back in place on top.

Geri shrieked, so did Marta.

"What was that?" Carmela asked.

"Don't let go!" Marta shouted. "Maintain the circle."

Henry looked suspiciously around. "That didn't sound like any ghost," he said.

"Sound?" Geri said. "I didn't hear nothing. But I kind of felt something."

"Me, too," Carmela said.

"Be quiet, Henry," Marta said. "Those two are

good. They feel her. Astrid is near."

"But I felt the whole table move," Henry said, clearly annoyed.

"Quiet, everyone. Breathe again, in unison. In … out," Marta said. "Is that you, Astrid? Are you with us?"

Silence.

"Come, spirit! I know you're here."

Again, nothing. Marta and Henry squeezed their eyes shut. Richie felt Marta's hand tighten so much on his he was surprised she had so much strength.

"Please, Grandmother!" Marta was all but begging. "Please tell me where the gold is! I need to know so I can escape. We need a way to live once we're out of the country."

"I'm here, child," a deep, breathless but ethereal voice called out.

Richie squinted, trying to see in the darkness. He was pretty sure the words had come from Geri. It seemed she had her head tossed back.

"Grandmother, is it you?" Marta's voice quavered.

"Yes." The voice was eerily different from

Geri's. This voice was higher and even lilting. "I didn't know I had a granddaughter. Why didn't you ever come to visit me?"

"I didn't know about you, or I would have," Marta cried. "I'm so sorry! My mother never told me. She believed you wanted to kill her."

"I never wanted to kill my own daughter."

"I know you didn't, Grandmother. Please tell me, where is the gold?"

"Leave it, and leave here. Danger is coming for you. Run, my dear."

"I'm not going anywhere without the gold, dammit!"

"You will not blaspheme in this house. Leave now."

"Look." Marta sounded peeved. "This is important to me. Now that you've learned you didn't kill your husband and daughter, you can go on to wherever ghosts go. You don't need to hang around this house anymore. That should be worth something to you, right? So how about you tell me where the gold is. One favor for another. Tit for tat, and all that. Okay?"

There was a long silence, and then the high,

sing-song voice said, "It's buried behind the barn."

"Barn?" Marta repeated. "Grandmother, there is no barn here."

"How could your great-grandfather run a dairy without a barn?"

"Oh," Marta said. "Henry, it must have been torn down. But a barn wouldn't be too far from the house. You'll have to find it."

"What if she's not telling you the truth?" Henry said.

"Why wouldn't she?" Marta asked.

"You don't believe me," Geri cried, still with her high, squeaky voice. "You're just like your grandfather! He never believed me either. I'm going."

"No! Wait."

"Goodbye."

"Grandmother! Astrid!"

Silence.

They all dropped their hands.

Henry pushed back the drapes to let sunlight into the room.

Marta glared at her husband. "Henry, you idiot!"

"All I wanted was some proof," he said.

"Yes, and you got my grandmother pissed off at us. Now go out there and find that barn."

"How am I supposed to know where it used to be?"

"Look for old boards, or maybe where the ground seems different from what's around it. How the hell should I know?"

He shook his head. "Maybe I need to get rid of them first. We don't need them anymore."

Richie and Rebecca eyed each other, trying to come up with something to stop them.

Marta stood up, her gun in hand. "What if it's hard to dig, or there's so much gold you need help loading it? We might need his help." She thrust her chin towards Richie. "Threaten to torture Momma, and he'll do whatever we want."

Henry nodded. "Good thinking."

"There's a shed on the far side of the house," Marta said. "It probably has some tools in there. Maybe a pick or a shovel you can use."

"Great." Henry grumbled his way out of the house.

Richie waited, shaking his head at Rebecca so

she wouldn't try anything foolish. Before long, they heard what sounded like a pick striking hard ground over and over.

"I guess he found where the barn used to be," Marta said with a smile. Seeing that her charges were docile, she took a seat, still holding the gun on them.

Richie caught Rebecca's eyes. He looked down at the table top, then up at her. She gave a small smile and nod.

With that, he put his hands on the edge of the table, and then stood as much as he was able to while tied to the chair. Rebecca did the same and together, in one quick motion, they lifted the table top, tipping it onto its side as they pushed it forward into Marta. The table knocked her backwards off her chair. She fired the gun, but the shot went wild. Her head hit the wall behind her, and the table landed on top of her legs.

At the same time, Richie slammed the legs of the chair he was tied to against a wall, splintering the old, dry wood on impact. The loosened ropes all but slid off his body.

He picked up the gun Marta had dropped as

she fell and then untied the knot at Rebecca's back and helped her pull off the ropes. He gave the gun to Rebecca.

The sound of the pick had stopped, and they both expected Henry to either come in or to shoot at them through the window.

Rebecca stood ready to fire if needed as Richie untied his mother and Geri, and then tied up Marta. Marta was dazed and crying with pain, saying her kneecaps had been smashed when the table fell onto them.

They ignored her.

All remained quiet outside.

"I'm going after Henry," Rebecca said. "You keep Carmela and Geri safe."

"They'll be fine waiting here. I'll be right behind you."

"No, Richie!" Carmela cried.

"She's not going out there alone." He aimed his words at Carmela, but knew they also told Rebecca not to waste her breath arguing.

Rebecca stood next to the dining-room door, Richie at her side. She reached out and opened the door a little way. She saw no movement or any change in the parlor. She opened the door wider and took a better look, then glanced back at Richie with a nod. The room was empty.

Slowly, her gun leading the way, Rebecca crossed the room. Richie looked around as he followed and even peeked out the window. He saw and heard nothing.

He wondered if Henry had run, leaving Marta behind.

As Rebecca edged her way to the front door, Richie stayed near the wall at her side.

She opened the door. When nothing happened, and no sound was heard, she slowly crept onto the front porch, looking over her shoulders and all around.

Richie inched towards the side of the house, then froze. A black Maserati sports car was parked under some trees. He took Rebecca's arm and nudged her closer to him. "Look."

They both peered around the corner of the house.

"What the hell?" she said as she lowered the gun.

Vito, holding a pick in his hand, stood near

Henry. Henry look like a stick figure alongside Vito's girth. Shay sat on an ancient barrel with his Smith and Wesson aimed at Henry.

"It's about time," Richie said, strolling off the porch and out to meet them. "I expected you a lot earlier."

"My biggest problem was to make sure I didn't blow past you on the highway." Shay nodded towards his sports car. "We didn't want anyone watching to know you weren't alone."

"You could have come inside and helped," Richie said.

"What, you couldn't take care of one little old lady by yourself?" Vito asked.

Richie just shook his head and went to get Carmela and Geri. Rebecca, he saw, was already heading inland, trying to pick up a signal on her cell phone to call the local authorities.

Chapter 24

Thank goodness I can go home soon," Carmela said as she got into the ambulance with Geri. The paramedics insisted they be checked out by a doctor in the hospital after their harrowing experiences, although both women knew they were just fine.

"You two really had them going," Richie said with a smile. "They believed you could communicate with spirits."

"You think we were joking?" Carmela asked, her expression serious.

Richie looked so stunned, Carmela and Geri both laughed at him for being taken so easily.

"Actually, I wanted to tell them the gold was in the outhouse," Geri said, "but I didn't think I could do it without laughing." She and Carmela now guffawed so hard they almost did need hospitalization. "We 'connected with spirits' the same way during séances, once we saw how they worked. We were afraid they'd realize we were faking, but they never questioned us at all."

"That's the trouble with people who believe in any new crackpot thing that comes along," Carmela said. "They're easy to convince."

"I decided to send Henry outside to get him away from Marta," Geri added. "I knew once they were separated, and Richie and Rebecca didn't need to spend all their time worrying about us, we'd get through this."

"Girl power," Carmela said and the two high-fived. But then she faced Rebecca and Richie. "We also want to apologize to both of you."

"No need," Rebecca said. "You didn't do this on purpose."

"In a sense, we did. Oh, not that we planned to get kidnapped or to put you in danger," Carmela hastened to explain. "But we should have let you know we suspected Henry and Marta as soon as we heard poor Sandy was dead."

"Are you kidding me?" Richie bellowed. "Why didn't you tell us? You could have been killed."

"We never dreamed everything would turn dangerous so fast," Carmela said. "At least you found us. How did you do it so quickly?"

Richie froze. "Uh … Rebecca was here once before."

He and Rebecca glanced at each other and both struggled not to grin.

The ambulance soon left with the two women plus Marta of the damaged kneecaps and her police escort, while Henry went straight to jail. More police and a local towing company were already dealing with Lucian's body and car down on the beach.

Vito and Shay had taken off in Shay's Maserati as soon as Rebecca went in search of a cell phone signal to call in law enforcement. Rebecca couldn't believe it when she saw their tail lights. She had no idea how she was supposed to account for them to the police.

A couple of detectives from San Mateo county were delayed. Rebecca and Richie agreed to wait for them to arrive to give them their statements. They were due within the half hour.

"Let's walk," Richie said. "Just the two of us before we need to talk to those detectives and then wait forever for the doctors to look over my mother and Geri. I'm going to try to get them to stay at my house tonight so they won't be alone and start thinking of the horrible things that *might* have happened to all of us. You can join us if you'd like."

"I think I'll skip that pleasure," she said, trying to keep a straight face. But she was glad to have some time alone with him. She had never thought of him as particularly brave before, but everything he did, from going into the warehouse to rescue Claire Baxter, to searching for a way down the cliff to try to save the occupants of Lucian's car, to attacking a woman holding a gun on him, made her see him as brave now. "I'll probably be at Homicide all night. I've got a few cases to clear."

As they walked away from the house to the north side of the small peninsula, far from the beach with Lucian's car, she pointed out the path down the hillside to the beach, the path she had taken with Geller.

"We did it," Richie said as they stood on the shore. "You and I. We saved them."

He sounded completely overjoyed. "Yes, we did," she said with a laugh.

As their gazes met, she saw joy and much more as he looked at her. Her breath caught. "Let's keep going." She turned away from him.

He quickly caught up and put his arm around her shoulders as they slowly ambled along the shoreline. "It's crazy," he said, "when you think about what started this whole mess. A bunch of people going to séances, looking to the past, looking backwards to live through loved ones who were gone. It makes sense it wouldn't turn out well."

"It was sad," she said.

"If at all possible, a person needs to look to the future. That's where there's hope—and life."

The thought struck her that he might be thinking about himself and his fiancée when he said that, whether he realized it or not.

"You're right," she murmured.

He dropped his arm and walked closer to the ocean. He picked up a piece of driftwood and flung it toward the water, watching with satisfaction at the distance he achieved.

She stepped to his side and put a hand on his shoulder. When he faced her, the raw emotion coming from him rolled over her like a wave. She was unnerved by what she saw, and what she felt for him. Unnerved because she knew, whatever she might be feeling, that the two of them as a couple would never work.

She dropped her hand and searched for what to say to bring things back to their usual casual relationship. "After seeing the pain losing a loved one brought to all those people who gave their money to Sandy, I guess I'm glad I'm not looking for that kind of deep relationship." When he made no reply, she added, "I suspect you feel the same way." She forced a smile. "There's much to be said for 'no strings.'"

He didn't reply for a moment as his gaze searched hers. "I think it wasn't the pain of loss that caused those people to fall into the Sandorista trap. The problem for them, what they couldn't deal with, was loneliness."

She hadn't expected that from him, and she realized he was right. They started to walk again, side-by-side, down the beach.

"It's good then," she said, trying once more, "that neither of us leads a boring life. We don't have time to be lonely."

"Busy people can still be lonely, Rebecca." He reached for her hand as they continued to skirt the water. His jaw tightened for a moment, and then he said, "But you're right. It's good we're busy."

She couldn't leave it at that, not after hearing the honest sadness in his words. "I must admit, I do find you a surprisingly good companion."

He glanced quizzically at her, but then his face slowly spread into a smile. "Good, because I find you the same. It's nice, you know, when two people find this ... what should we call it? Companionship."

She felt suddenly empty inside. "Yes. Of course. That's what it is." They walked along the sandy beach until they reached a stretch of rocks that headed out into the water.

Richie climbed up onto the rocks and helped Rebecca join him. She did, and the two of them walked nearer to the water, and then sat. Waves gently rolled up onto the rocks a little way below their feet.

"It's beautiful here," he said.

Their shoulders touched, and she could feel the

warmth in his dark eyes as he faced her.

"Yes. I wish we could stay here a long time."

"I'd like it," he said.

Despite her caution, she couldn't help but to lean a little closer to him as they watched and listened to the waves lap against the shore.

But soon he looked towards the house. The county detectives stood at the top of the hill waiting for them.

Behind the detectives, the house seemed oddly brighter than it had before, as if some darkness, perhaps some sadness, had been lifted from it.

"Come on, Inspector," Richie said, holding out his hand to help her climb back down onto the sand. "Your duty awaits."

Chapter 25

Rebecca woke with a start to the sound of her cell phone buzzing. The first thing she thought was that it was the dispatcher calling, but then she remembered that her on-call shift had ended.

After leaving Half Moon Bay, she had worked most of that night and again all day Friday on Geller and Lucian's deaths, as well as doing all she could to make sure the cases against Henry and Marta Highfield were airtight. She and Richie had managed to convince the San Mateo detectives that she had given the "mystery men"—Shay and Vito—approval to leave since they weren't needed for the case. She ended up chewed out by Lt. Eastwood for that—what else was new?—but she found it better than possibly opening Shay up to more scrutiny, especially if the FBI got wind of his identity.

More important was the jurisdictional issue between San Francisco and San Mateo counties, but by late Friday night when, exhausted, she went home, she was pretty sure she'd get the case.

She had talked to Richie briefly about his statements and was glad to hear Carmela and Geri were doing just fine.

Now, she sat up in bed and reached for the phone. First she saw the caller: Richie. Then the time: 3:00 a.m.

"Hello?" she mumbled.

"If you're alone, open your front door. It's raining." Then he hung up.

It took her a moment to process what he had said, and then she got out of bed. She was wearing her old yellow cotton pajamas, three big buttons kept the top closed, and an elastic waistband held up the bottoms. She went to the door.

He was standing there in the rain, his eyes troubled and questioning. "I know this is crazy, but—"

"Come inside," she said.

He walked into the apartment.

"What's wrong?" she asked.

He ran his hand through his damp hair and then brushed some raindrops off his jacket. "Put on shoes. Or slippers. It doesn't matter which. And a

304 | Joanne Pence

coat."

"Shouldn't I get dressed first?"

He couldn't help but smile as he looked at her pj's. "They're fine. Hurry."

"Hurry?" She did as he asked. Something—a sixth sense?—told her to go along, or she might always regret it. She put on her leather jacket. "Why?"

He lifted Spike and put him in her arms, then found a couple cans of Spike's food and put them in his pockets. He picked up her handbag, added her badge, gun, and cell phone, and then took her hand and pulled her outside the apartment.

"What are you doing?" she demanded as she watched him make sure both doors were locked. "It's cold and wet out here."

"It's warm and dry in the car."

She and Spike got in. "Now will you tell me what this is about?" she asked.

"You'll see soon enough."

He tore across the city. The streets were all but empty, and he didn't even bother to wait for red lights to change once he saw no cars were coming. It was as if they were the only people out and about in the city.

Rebecca soon realized he was heading for his house. And it was clear he wasn't about to answer any of her questions, so she just stared at him as he drove, wondering what madness had overtaken him.

He pulled into the garage. They walked up the stairs to the door that opened to his kitchen. She envied his kitchen—large, attractive and modern with white cabinets and pale blue, gray, and white granite countertops. If she ever had time to cook, which she rarely did, she'd love a kitchen like this one to work in.

She put Spike down. Richie opened the back door, and Spike trotted out. He left the back door open for Spike's return as he put a bowl with water on the floor for him. In thirty seconds flat, Spike was back inside, shaking off the rain.

Richie finally faced Rebecca.

She wondered if he'd explain. "Now, will you—"

He took her handbag from her arm, placed it on the counter, and then led her into the living room. The living room was dominated by a picture window. From his home near the top of Twin Peaks the city lights far below were like a sparkling carpet, interrupted by lit spires of tall buildings. Beyond the downtown, the outline of the Bay Bridge was like a Christmas decoration spanning the bay.

The living room had a cozy warmth, with a light gray sectional, two blue chairs, coffee and lamp tables of pale ash, a fire place, and a 60-inch plasma TV.

He helped her out of her coat and placed it on the sofa, then removed his jacket and tossed it beside hers. He flicked a switch to light his fireplace. "Would you like some wine?"

"No." She gawked at him.

"Good." He put his arms around her.

She drew back, her hands on his arms. "What is this? Have you gone crazy?"

"No. Sane. It's time to finish what we started months ago—the last time you were here. We would have back then, except my mother showed up."

"And now she's not here?" Rebecca's pulse pounded. Well did she remember—almost too well—how it had felt holding him, kissing him, the last time she was in this room.

"No. She and her friend both wanted to sleep in their own beds tonight, thank God. So she won't be interrupting this time."

"This time?"

"She was a little crazy back then with worry, and I was a little crazy with a different kind of worry—about you. I tried to walk away from you. And that made me even crazier."

"I don't—"

"Don't you?"

He drew her close, and this time she let him. But instead of moving faster, everything slowed. She could feel the heat from his hands against the thin cotton of her night clothes.

"Tell me to take you back home," he murmured. "Tell me you never want to see me again, and I'll do as you ask. And I'll promise to never bother you again. Never."

She couldn't do that.

She lifted a hand to his head, her fingers twining in his hair. She loved the feel of it, soft, and wavy. A part of her was tempted to give it a good hard yank, to hurt him for having hurt her when he ignored her for so long, but much more than that, she wanted him, and had for a long time.

She let go of his hair, and studied his face, a face she had come to know well over the course of one bit of craziness after the other that she had been through with him. And perhaps the craziest thing of all was how much she had come to care about him.

Her eyes never left his as she pulled his shirt free of his belt, lifting it and his undershirt so that her cool hands could touch his warm skin. As soon as they did, his mouth found hers. She pressed her body closer as their kisses grew fiercer, hungrier. He started moving forward, towards her, and she stepped backwards even as she kept him close. She knew where he was headed and pulled him along every bit as much as he was pushing her.

His fingers found the buttons on her pajama top, and he opened them while she struggled with his first button. At that same moment, the back of her legs bumped the bed.

In no time they were atop it, their clothes in a heap on the floor.

She had found out once before that she loved

the way he kissed, but she learned those kisses had been nothing compared to the way he made her feel now.

He surprised her, somehow knowing how to hold her, kiss her, touch her; how to make the conflagration that was her body grow even hotter.

He overwhelmed her, and she loved it.

When their breathing became steady once more, and their heartbeats calmed, he rolled onto his back and then reached for her hand, lacing his fingers between hers. "I always thought," he murmured, "that making love with you would be special, but I never imagined …"

She liked hearing that. And for this moment, at least, her heart filled with … emotion … for him, with more feelings than she ever wanted or suspected. She did what she could to tamp them down. But despite her caution, she couldn't resist leaning forward and kissing his lips, his cheeks, his aquiline nose, and what she always thought of as his "Al Pacino" eyes.

"What are you doing?" he asked with a smile.

She leaned back and drew her finger from his ear to his jawline, to his neck, and shoulder. "I wish

I knew," she whispered, a little frightened by the amount of emotion she heard in her voice, and realizing he heard it, too. "But I know it's something I've wanted to do for a long, long time."

"Good," he said. Then he rose up and flipped her onto her back as he took her in his arms once more.

oOo

Much later, she opened her eyes. It was still dark outside, but the living room lamp had been left on, and cast the bedroom in a soft glow. The red numbers of the clock-radio on the nightstand read 5:23 A.M. Spike was curled up at the foot of the bed. She looked over her shoulder and there, beside her, lay Richie, sound asleep.

She turned to face him. Sleeping, his hair tousled and falling onto his forehead, he looked completely angelic. She listened to the deep, steady rhythm of his breathing. The pillow beneath her head carried his scent, and she liked it. She liked everything about being here with him.

And that's what worried her.

Her relationships had always turned out badly, which meant chances were that eventually they'd part. As much as he might be wrong for her, she feared she was even worse for him. After losing a fiancée, the last thing he needed was a fly-by-night affair. He needed someone who could always be there with him. Someone who would make all those foods with long names that ended in i's and a's that she couldn't begin to pronounce let alone cook. Someone who could see to it that he stopped getting involved with dangerous people like smugglers of ancient artifacts.

Someone she could never be.

If she was smart, while he slept, she would gather up her clothes and her dog, call a taxi, and leave. And yet, she hated the thought of not seeing him again. Of not feeling the excitement that always filled her whenever he was near.

As she watched him sleep, as she felt him easing his way into her very protected heart, she couldn't help but to move a little closer to him. His heavy-lidded eyes opened. "Good morning," he mumbled, and then he quickly went back to sleep.

She smiled.

Listening to her head, she would tiptoe from the room and go back home. But listening to her heart ...

She snuggled deeper under the blankets and, as sleep overtook her and her eyes drifted shut, the thought struck that although she had no idea where this would lead, she could be certain of one thing: it was going to be an interesting journey. And it was one that she didn't want to miss.

Plus ...

Don't miss hearing about the next Rebecca and Richie story, and all of Joanne's new books by signing up for her mailing list at www.joannepence.com.

*Find out what happens next in the lives of Rebecca and Richie when the clock strikes **Four**.*

Here's the beginning of ***Four O'Clock Sizzle***:

San Francisco Fire Department Captain Warren Eisen, head of the Bureau of Fire Investigations, believed arson was the cause of the early morning blaze that gutted the storeroom of Easy Street Clothiers. It was an upscale store that catered to hip young men as well as older men hoping to appear "cool," and willing to pay a fortune for jeans, shirts, and jackets that looked well-worn when purchased. No three-piece suit, necktie or, God forbid, a bow tie would ever darken

314 | Joanne Pence

the racks of Easy Street.

If the cause of the fire was arson, the death of the man found in the store would very likely be ruled a homicide.

What Homicide Inspector Rebecca Mayfield found strange, however, was that when she and her partner Bill Sutter arrived at the scene, Easy Street Clothier's owner, Diego Bosque, had already gone. He put his store manager, Dan Peters, in charge. The detectives tried to locate Bosque, but he wasn't answering his phone, or heeding their voice message requests to return to the building.

No one, as yet, knew the identity of the victim. He was found curled on the floor of the storeroom as if asleep, an empty bottle of what is often called "Two Buck Chuck" next to him. He was white, probably in his forties or fifties, thin and malnourished. Judging from his clothes—definitely not Easy Street quality—he appeared to be a derelict who had somehow gotten inside with his wine and died of smoke inhalation while he slept. Very likely, no one knew he was there when the fire alarms went off.

After spending the morning talking to

neighboring store owners and others who worked nearby, and obtaining information on the employees, Rebecca returned to the Hall of Justice to run some employee names through the system to see if any red flags turned up. At the same time, Bill Sutter was doing what he could to run down the name of the victim.

The Homicide Bureau was located on the Hall's fourth floor. It consisted of a large, open main room crammed with inspectors' desks and filing cabinets, books, and computers. Off it were interview rooms, and nearby was the office of the chief, Lt. James Philip Eastwood.

As Rebecca entered the bureau, she was surprised to see three of homicide's detectives, Bo Benson, Paavo Smith, and Luis Calderon, huddled around the secretary's desk. Whatever Elizabeth Havlin was showing them was causing them to laugh like a group of teenage boys pouring over their first copy of *Playboy*. Rebecca headed their way.

"What's going on?" she asked.

"Oh!" Elizabeth cried. She shut the magazine they were looking at and flipped it over, face-down.

Rebecca caught a glimpse of the cover: *San Francisco Beat.* It was a weekly pulp rag filled with mostly scurrilous stories about the Bay Area's rich and famous. Elizabeth's whole face turned bright red. "Look!" she pointed to a vase of roses on a side table. "They just came for you. Must be a secret admirer."

"For me?" Rebecca was surprised. The roses were beautiful.

The three detectives all but ran back to their desks. Rebecca glanced at them as she pulled out the note. *May these help brighten your Monday. — Richie.*

She smiled. How sweet! She couldn't even remember the last time anyone sent her flowers. And never at work. She wondered if speculation about her flowers was what the "boys" as she called the male detectives she worked with—and sometimes they did act like boys—had been chuckling over.

"Or, maybe they came from a not-so-secret admirer?" Elizabeth said with a knowing smile.

Rebecca's lips pursed. She didn't like the thought of anyone at work knowing about her private life. Especially not when it involved Richie Amalfi. It was bad enough that he was the cousin of the wife of her co-worker, Homicide Inspector Paavo Smith, but she always felt, sadly, that despite liking him a whole lot, that theirs was no "forever" relationship. They'd have a pleasant fling, but eventually each would go their separate ways. So she didn't want people she worked with to think more was going on here than actually was. "It's no one you know," she said curtly. Sometimes a white lie was better than truthfully saying, "It's none of your business."

"I see." Elizabeth gave a forced laugh.

Rebecca wondered why Elizabeth was acting so strangely, noticing she now had her arms crossed atop the magazine as if desperately trying to hide it.

"May I see?" Rebecca asked, holding out her hand. While most people would think they needed to "respect" Elizabeth's desire to hide the magazine, as a cop, Rebecca had learned to ask for and get what she wanted, when she wanted it.

"Oh, you don't want to look at it," Elizabeth said, nervously shaking her head. "It's a sleazy tabloid, that's all. Nothing but lies—gossip and lies. You can't believe a thing you read in it."

"I know that," Rebecca said. "It's why I never read it. But I'd like to be in on the joke."

Elizabeth drew in a deep breath. "Before I give it to you, I've got to explain. I had no idea what was in it. I only bought it for fun."

"Okay," Rebecca murmured, more puzzled than ever. And then like a beat cop who was tired of pussy-footing around, she said, "Hand it over."

Elizabeth handed over the magazine.

The cover screamed, *"San Francisco's Bad Boys: The City's 6 Most Enticing Bachelors."* On that cover was a montage of six good-looking men. And among them, smiling at the camera in a full, toothy grin, was the guy who had just gifted her with beautiful roses, Richie Amalfi himself. "Oh, shit!"

Rebecca usually made it a point not to swear because she'd grown so sick of the constant barrage of foul language she heard on the streets as a cop. But this time, she couldn't help herself.

"Don't …" Elizabeth cleared her throat. "Don't bother to read it. It's garbage."

Rebecca flipped to the article. She actually was tempted to give the rag back to Elizabeth when her eye caught the name of another "bad boy." Diego Bosque, the hard-to-reach owner of Easy Street Clothiers.

Without saying a word, she took her roses and the magazine and headed to her desk. Watching her, the other detectives, Bo, Paavo, and Luis, looked ready to crawl under their own desks. One-by-one, each skedaddled out of the bureau. She was getting a very bad feeling about this. She sat down, stiffened her shoulders and began to read.

Our six bachelors aren't the Bay Area's richest men and not necessarily the most handsome. And yet, through force of personality combined with renown in their respective fields, everyone notices when one of these bad boys enters a room. And if you don't believe us, just listen to what the women—and a few men—who best know our six 'Enticing Bachelors' have to say.

Continue with *Four O'Clock Sizzler* wherever fine ebooks and print books are sold.

About the Author

Joanne Pence was born and raised in northern California. She has been an award-winning, *USA Today* best-selling author of mysteries for many years, but she has also written historical fiction, contemporary romance, romantic suspense, a fantasy, and supernatural suspense. All of her books are now available as ebooks, and most are also in print. Joanne hopes you'll enjoy her books, which present a variety of times, places, and reading experiences, from mysterious to thrilling, emotional to lightly humorous, as well as powerful tales of times long past.

Visit her at www.joannepence.com and be sure to sign up for Joanne's mailing list to hear about new books.

The Rebecca Mayfield Mysteries

Rebecca is a by-the-book detective, who walks the straight and narrow in her work, and in her life.

Richie, on the other hand, is not at all by-the-book. But opposites can and do attract, and there are few mystery two-somes quite as opposite as Rebecca and Richie.

ONE O'CLOCK HUSTLE – North American Book Award winner in Mystery

TWO O'CLOCK HEIST

THREE O'CLOCK SÉANCE

FOUR O'CLOCK SIZZLE

FIVE O'CLOCK TWIST

SIX O'CLOCK SILENCE

Plus a Christmas Novella: The Thirteenth Santa

The Angie & Friends Food & Spirits Mysteries

Angie Amalfi and Homicide Inspector Paavo Smith are soon to be married in this latest mystery series. Crime and calories plus a new "twist" in Angie's life in the form of a ghostly family inhabiting the house she and Paavo buy, create a mystery series with a "spirited" sense of fun and adventure.

COOKING SPIRITS
ADD A PINCH OF MURDER
COOK'S BIG DAY
MURDER BY DEVIL'S FOOD
Plus a Christmas mystery-fantasy: COOK'S CURIOUS CHRISTMAS
And a cookbook: COOK'S DESSERT COOKBOOK

The early "Angie Amalfi mystery series" began when Angie first met San Francisco Homicide Inspector Paavo Smith. Here are those mysteries in the order written:
SOMETHING'S COOKING
TOO MANY COOKS
COOKING UP TROUBLE
COOKING MOST DEADLY
COOK'S NIGHT OUT
COOKS OVERBOARD
A COOK IN TIME
TO CATCH A COOK
BELL, COOK, AND CANDLE
IF COOKS COULD KILL
TWO COOKS A-KILLING

COURTING DISASTER
RED HOT MURDER
THE DA VINCI COOK

Supernatural Suspense

Ancient Echoes
Top Idaho Fiction Book Award Winner

Over two hundred years ago, a covert expedition shadowing Lewis and Clark disappeared in the wilderness of Central Idaho. Now, seven anthropology students and their professor vanish in the same area. The key to finding them lies in an ancient secret, one that men throughout history have sought to unveil.

Michael Rempart is a brilliant archeologist with a colorful and controversial career, but he is plagued by a sense of the supernatural and a spiritual intuitiveness. Joining Michael are a CIA consultant on paranormal phenomena, a washed-up local sheriff, and a former scholar of Egyptology. All must overcome their personal demons as they attempt to save the students and learn the expedition's terrible secret....

Ancient Shadows

One by one, a horror film director, a judge, and a newspaper publisher meet brutal deaths. A link exists between them, and the deaths have only begun ....

Archeologist Michael Rempart finds himself pitted against ancient demons and modern conspirators when a dying priest gives him a powerful artifact—a pearl said to have granted Genghis Khan the power, eight centuries ago, to lead his Mongol warriors across the steppes to the gates of Vienna.

The artifact has set off centuries of war and destruction as it conjures demons to play upon men's strongest ambitions and cruelest desires. Michael realizes the so-called pearl is a philosopher's stone, the prime agent of alchemy. As much as he would like to ignore the artifact, when he sees horrific deaths and experiences, first-hand, diabolical possession and affliction, he has no choice but to act, to follow a path along the Old Silk Road to a land that time forgot, and to somehow find a place that may no longer exist in the world as he knows it.

Historical, Contemporary & Fantasy Romance

Dance with a Gunfighter

Gabriella Devere wants vengeance. She grows up quickly when she witnesses the murder of her family by a gang of outlaws, and vows to make them pay for their crime. When the law won't help her, she takes matters into her own hands.

Jess McLowry left his war-torn Southern home to head West, where he hired out his gun. When he learns what happened to Gabriella's family, and what she plans, he knows a young woman like her will have no chance against the outlaws, and vows to save her the way he couldn't save his own family.

But the price of vengeance is high and Gabriella's willingness to sacrifice everything ultimately leads to the book's deadly and startling conclusion.

Willa Cather Literary Award finalist for Best Historical Novel.

The Dragon's Lady

Turn-of-the-century San Francisco comes to life in this romance of star-crossed lovers whose love is forbidden by both society and the laws of the time.

Ruth Greer, wealthy daughter of a shipping magnate, finds a young boy who has run away from his home in Chinatown—an area of gambling parlors, opium dens, and sing-song girls, as well as families trying to eke out a living. It is also home to the infamous and deadly "hatchet men" of Chinese lore.

There, Ruth meets Li Han-lin, a handsome, enigmatic leader of one such tong, and discovers he is neither as frightening cruel, or wanton as reputation would have her believe. As Ruth's fascination with the lawless area grows, she finds herself pulled deeper into its intrigue and dangers, particularly those surrounding Han-lin. But the two are from completely different worlds, and when both worlds are shattered by the Great Earthquake and Fire of 1906 that destroyed most of San Francisco, they face their ultimate test.

Seems Like Old Times

When Lee Reynolds, nationally known television news anchor, returns to the small town where she was born to sell her now-vacant childhood home, little does she expect to find that her first love has moved back to town. Nor does she expect that her feelings .for him are still so strong.

Tony Santos had been a major league baseball player, but now finds his days of glory gone. He's gone back home to raise his young son as a single dad.

Both Tony and Lee have changed a lot. Yet, being with him, she finds that in her heart, it seems like old times...

The Ghost of Squire House

For decades, the home built by reclusive artist, Paul Squire, has stood empty on a windswept cliff overlooking the ocean. Those who attempted to live in the home soon fled in terror. Jennifer Barrett knows nothing of the history of the house she inherited. All she knows is she's glad for the chance to make a new life for herself.

It's Paul Squire's duty to rid his home of intruders, but something about this latest newcomer's vulnerable status ... and resemblance of someone from his past ... dulls his resolve. Jennifer would like to find a real flesh-and-blood man to liven her days and nights—someone to share her life with—but living in the artist's house, studying his paintings, she is surprised at how close she feels to him.

A compelling, prickly ghost with a tortured, guilt-ridden past, and a lonely heroine determined to start fresh, find themselves in a battle of wills and emotion in this ghostly fantasy of love, time, and chance.

Dangerous Journey

C.J. Perkins is trying to find her brother who went missing while on a Peace Corps assignment in Asia. All she knows is that the disappearance has something to do with a "White Dragon." Darius Kane, adventurer and bounty hunter, seems to be her only hope, and she practically shanghais him into helping her.

With a touch of the romantic adventure film Romancing the Stone, C.J. and Darius follow a trail that takes them through the narrow streets of Hong Kong, the backrooms of San Francisco's Chinatown, and the wild jungles of Borneo as they pursue both her brother and the White Dragon. The closer C.J. gets to them, the more danger she finds herself in—and it's not just danger of losing her life, but also of losing her heart.